Higher Love

Alexandria House

Pink Cashmere Publishing, LLC

Arkansas, USA

Printed in the United States of America

First Printing 2017

ISBN: 0-9971461-9-2
ISBN-13: 978-0-9971461-9-6

Pink Cashmere Publishing, LLC
pinkcashmerepub@gmail.com
http://pinkcashmerepublishing.webs.com/

For *him*.

Higher Love

Popular travel blogger, Greer Kennedy, is living the good life with a successful career and equally as successful fiancé until one phone call from a friend opens her eyes to the truth of her relationship.

Tall, gorgeous, and successful in his own right, Derek Hill is dealing with some serious relationship problems as well.

When their paths cross, they mutually, but unofficially, decide to share a night—or three or four—of anonymous pleasure. Will they end up experiencing much more than either of them bargained for?

1

Greer

I was running late.

In less than three hours I had to be at the airport. Yet, there I stood, rifling through my closet, still undecided about what I was taking with me on this trip, as if taking trips was something I didn't do all the time. I sighed as I tossed another rejected outfit onto the bed next to my suitcase. At this rate, I would never make it to the airport on time.

I turned and grabbed a floral skater dress from a hanger, held it in front of me, and stared at myself in the mirror. Deciding it was appropriate summer music festival wear, I folded it and placed it at the bottom of the cavernous suitcase.

One down. At least five more to go. I liked having several outfit options when I traveled.

Next, I chose a white peasant blouse and a pair of distressed denim shorts, an electric blue harem-style jumpsuit, my favorite dashiki that I paired with some black skinny jeans, a multicolored maxi dress, my turquoise bikini, and a black flouncy mini skirt. I had already packed my toiletries. The only thing left would be deciding which shoes and accessories to take, which would be an equally daunting task.

I'd almost forgotten about packing underwear and was tossing some into my bag when my cell began to ring. Seeing that it was my friend, Trevia, I rolled my eyes and shook my head. This was the third time she'd called in less than an hour, and I just didn't have time for her theatrics and gossip. At least not until I was settled at my gate.

She called for the fourth time when I was in my car on my way to the airport, and since traffic was backed up, I answered, hoping whatever was so urgent would help me pass the time and keep my mind off of the possibility of missing my flight.

Before I could say hello, "Why haven't you been answering your phone?" was being screamed into my ear.

"Because I was trying to get ready for this trip. And stop yelling. What's up?"

"*You* tell *me*."

I sighed. "Trevia, come on. What is going on? Why've you been blowing up my phone?"

"Did you listen to my messages?"

"Obviously not. What is it?"

"I can't believe you'd keep something like this from me, G. I cannot believe it! We've been friends since high school, talked each other off the ledge after some pretty bad break-ups, and you didn't call me? I'm hurt. I'm really, really hurt."

I inched forward on the highway and slapped the steering wheel of my car. "Trevia Diann McCall! What the hell are you talking about?! What didn't I tell you?!"

"Well, either your man's Facebook is hacked or you two broke up."

I frowned as I stopped my violet VW Bug for the thousandth time. "What are you talking about? I talked to him last night. We're fine."

There was silence, and then, "Oh…my bad. I guess he got hacked then. You better let him know."

As the traffic began to pick up a little, I relaxed in my seat. "So all of this marathon calling was over some Facebook nonsense? You've got to get a grip, Trevia."

"Whatever. Be careful and have fun on your trip. Get a video of Maxwell for me."

"I'll do my best. Any other requests?"

"Nope, that's it. Sorry about…well, you know."

"Mm-hmm. I'll talk to you later, crazy ass."

I ended the call and dialed my fiancé, Lloyd's, number. Since he was at work, I wasn't surprised when it went straight to voicemail. "Hey, babe. It's Greer. I'm on my way to the airport and wanted to tell you what Trevia's crazy butt just called me with. I'll call you when I get to Virginia. Love you. Bye."

I coasted the rest of the way to the airport and made it right on time.

*****

My room at the Embassy Suites was even nicer than expected, but that was probably because I dropped the fact that I was a travel blogger on the front desk clerk and an upgrade appeared out of thin air. Funny how often that happened to me.

I rolled my suitcase into the closet and plopped down on the bed. My room offered a decent view of the city, and the king-sized bed seemed comfortable enough, but this was one of those times when my job felt a little lonely. I knew I'd enjoy the Neo Soul Festival better if my friends or my man were with me, but everyone either had other plans or had to work. For Lloyd, it was work. Well, it was always work with him, not that I was complaining. He earned a great living working in corporate compliance at Adventure Airlines, and that was definitely a plus since I was marrying him in a year or so. We hadn't quite settled on a date yet.

I grabbed my phone, decided to call and see if he'd at least talk dirty to me. I smiled as the phone rang in my ear. The smile evaporated from my face when I got his voicemail again. "Hey, it's me again. I'm in Virginia missing you. Call me back. Show starts at seven tonight, so call me before then. Love you. Bye." I rolled over, stared at the ceiling, and before I knew it, had fallen asleep.

2

Greer

I woke up later than I planned to, had to jump in and out of the shower and dress in less than thirty minutes, but still made it to the huge park that served as the festival's venue early enough to check out the vendors and get some great pictures for my blog and my Instagram page. I'd been blogging my travel adventures for years and thanks to a huge following, blogging became a full-time career for me two years earlier. Every year I set a theme for my adventures. This year it was festivals.

I found a spot near the center of the park, spread out the beautiful Kente-print blanket I'd just purchased from a vendor, and took a seat. I had just bitten into my foot-long corndog slathered with mustard when I heard a voice say, "Is this spot taken?"

I looked up to see a vision in smooth chocolate standing to my left—tall, fine, dreadlocks, gold stud in his ear, deep-set dark eyes, nice bone structure, gorgeous white smile, handsome as hell—pointing to a spot of grass. If I hadn't been a taken woman, I might have pulled my maxi dress up and flashed him some leg, because looking as good as he looked, he deserved a peek. He really did. "Not that I know of," I said after I swallowed my food.

"Good, this jerk chicken is calling my name." He held up a Styrofoam container.

My eyes widened. How the hell did I miss the jerk chicken? "I bet it is," I replied.

He'd opened his mouth to respond when a woman approached. "I've been looking all over for you!" she said.

He gave me another smile before turning his attention to her. She said something about finding them a better spot and then led him away. He tossed me a little wave before leaving with her.

*****

It was 9:00 PM when that evening's headliner, Bilal, took the stage. I was feeling myself, swaying with raised arms to *Soul Sista* when I felt someone tap me on my shoulder—fine-chocolate-dreadlocks was back. I frowned slightly as he leaned in to whisper in my ear, the warmth of his breath brushing against my skin, tickling it a bit. "Hey, I didn't catch your name earlier."

"I didn't throw it," I shouted.

"I know, I mean—" he proffered me his hand, "I'm Derek."

"That's nice. What's your wife's name?"

"Wife?"

I shook my head. "Have a great evening," I said, then closed my eyes and resumed swaying to the music. I hoped he'd get the message that I was not interested in having some extramarital Neo Soul Festival affair with him. I had a man, a good, gainfully employed, unmarried but promised to me, man. I didn't open my eyes until two songs later. Fine-chocolate-dreadlocks was gone.

*****

I called Lloyd again on the Uber ride back to the hotel, and that call went straight to voicemail, too. He also hadn't called me back. It wasn't like Lloyd not to check on me when I was out of town, and I was beginning to worry. Maybe there was something to this whole Facebook hacking thing, and maybe that wasn't the only thing that was hacked. Maybe he was dealing with some major damage from someone getting his financial information or worse. A crisis like that would be big enough for him to neglect me.

Once in my hotel room, I fired up my laptop and sent him an email, then I decided to check his Facebook page out of curiosity only to find that it had been deleted.

3

Greer

I called Lloyd again over breakfast.

Still no answer.

I was seconds away from calling his mother when Trevia's name appeared on the screen of my cell phone. "Hey," I said, after accepting the call.

"Hey, what's wrong? You don't sound right."

"It's Lloyd. I can't get in touch with him, and his Facebook page is gone. I think something serious might be going on with him."

"You want me to go by his place and check on him?"

"No, no…I don't want you to do that." I sighed. "I think I'm gonna call his mom and see if she's heard from him. Or maybe I'll call his friend Kareem…"

"Yeah, I'm on Facebook now and his page *is* gone. That's so weird. I wonder…"

"What?"

"Well, one time I got into it with my sister, Jayla, and she changed the privacy settings on her page, blocking me. I couldn't find it but it still existed."

"You think Lloyd did that?"

"Girl, no. I was just thinking out loud. Why would he change his privacy settings and block you, of all people, from seeing him?"

I shrugged. "I don't know, but something is going on. Look, let me call you back later."

"Okay, bye."

I sat there for a few minutes, trying to decide if I really wanted to call his mother yet and worry her; then my phone rang again. Trevia.

"Hello?" I breathed into the phone.

"Hey, um…I was able to see Lloyd's page…"

"You were? How? Wait, there *is* a page? I mean, he still has one?"

"Yeah, my sister is over here and she logged in to her account and I was able to see his page through hers. It looks exactly the same, so I guess he must've just blocked you and me."

"Blocked? Why? We just talked the day before yesterday and everything was fine."

"Greer, are you sure everything was fine?"

"What do you mean? Of course I'm sure." I leaned forward in my chair and rested my elbows on the table. "What is going on?"

"I think I might've found the answer to that on his page."

"Okay…"

"Um, it says he's engaged."

"Yeah, to *me*."

"No, to someone named Tami."

4

Greer

I don't remember hanging up the phone or taking a shower or getting dressed or riding to the festival. All I know is I found myself standing on the grass in the middle of the park with the sounds of bass, guitar, drums, and people talking and laughing filling my ears. Various food aromas infiltrated my nose. The air around me was balmy and thick. I felt out of place, like I'd been dropped there from a time machine. I was confused and hurt, but I couldn't bring myself to call him again. He was obviously ignoring my calls for Tami.

Who the hell was Tami?

What the hell happened to us? To me and Lloyd?

I sat right where I'd been standing, folded my legs Indian-style, and thought about the first time I saw him—tall and trim with light brown skin and hazel eyes. It was two years ago, and I had spent fifteen minutes studying the back of his body as I stood in line at the Apple store where we were both waiting to snatch up their next gen cell phone. He was wearing jeans and a khaki blazer, undoubtedly for casual Friday.

He smelled heavenly with his closely-cropped hair. I willed him to turn around, and when he did, I was sold. He was so handsome, so neat, so...*everything.* The man of my dreams.

He liked what he saw, too. Asked me out right then and there. Asked me to marry him a year later during a party at his mom's house. I'd always thought our whole relationship was so...serendipitous.

And now this.

Tami.

And *my* Lloyd.

But Tami who?

Maybe Facebook autocorrected Greer to Tami, I pondered. Then I decided that notion was stupid as hell. He'd dumped me without dumping me. He'd moved on without bothering to inform be that I'd been left behind.

What. An. Asshole.

I glanced around at the brown bodies surrounding me and spotted a woman sipping on something that appeared to be alcoholic. I think I startled her when I approached her and asked where she got it, because she didn't hesitate to tell me she'd brought it with her, whip out a clear plastic cup, and pour me some. Well, either that or my jilted ass just looked like I needed a drink.

I don't even know what it was, but it burned my throat and eased my anxiety if only just a little. Another shot and a plate of ribs later, I was right and ready for the main attraction of day two of the festival— the incomparable Angie Stone. The only problem was when I teleported to the park, I'd done so without my camera. My cell phone would have to do if I wanted pictures or videos.

My phone.

I dialed Lloyd's number, waited for it to go to voicemail, and then blurted, "I know you're screening your damn calls, you coward-ass bastard! You blocked me on Facebook like I'm some stalker? Screw your red ass! Screw you *and* Tami! Yeah, I know about her, too! I hope your little thing falls off! By the way, you sucked in bed. Sucked! You got no damn rhythm! It was like screwing a wooden block! No, it was worse than that! I can make the wooden block do what I need it to do! But your ass? You couldn't please a woman with a gun pointed at your head!"

Satisfied, I ended the call and fell onto my back in the grass. It was then that I noticed fine-chocolate-dreadlocks standing over me. "The hell you want? You lose your wife?" I spat.

"Uh, damn, I just got here, and I wasn't on the other end of that call."

I rolled my eyes, sat up and put my little cup up to my mouth, trying to make more liquor materialize. "I know that. What do you want?"

"Look, she's not my wife. She's my brother's wife. They're standing right over there. We ain't all dogs. At least I'm not."

I turned in the direction he was pointing to and saw the woman from the previous night with a guy who was almost but not quite as fine as him. He was also missing the dreadlocks. "Oh..."

I watched as he took a seat beside me. Angie was singing *Brotha,* and the crowd was vibing with her. "You okay?" he asked.

I glanced down at the lovely engagement ring I hadn't had the presence of mind to snatch off my finger, and thought, *Hell no*, but said, "Me? I couldn't be better. Footloose and fancy-damn-free."

He grinned. "You gonna tell me your name, Ms. Footloose?"

"What do you think my name is?"

"Hmmm, you look like a Monique."

"Then that's my name."

He scoffed. "Okay…well, I saw you over here and thought I'd come say hi and clear things up."

"That you did."

"All right. Enjoy the rest of the show, the rest of the festival, the rest of your life..." Whatever he said after that was unintelligible to me. He was probably calling me a bitter bitch or something similar. I couldn't argue with him if he was.

When he stood to leave, I got an eyeful of his firm butt and said, "Wait. Um, I'm sorry for being the way I've been being. It's just that…look, you can sit here if you want. I'd rather not be alone right now." It was the truth, but I wasn't sure why I'd admitted it to him. That liquor was doing strange things to me.

"You sure?" he asked.

I nodded. "Yeah."

In the middle of *Wish I Didn't Miss You,* I broke down. While everyone else was moving to the beat, Mr. Dreadlocks wrapped an arm around my shoulder. Before I realized what I was doing, I leaned into him and let my tears flow, sure that I had ruined both of our nights.

*****

"We riding out or what? Because I'm ready!"

I held the phone from my ear as my friend, Denise, continued shouting into the other end. Denise and Trevia and I had been friends forever. We met in the same band class years ago in high school, and I knew them both as well as I knew myself. While Trevia McCall liked to stir up mess, Denise Buhari loved to finish it. Trevia was all talk. Denise was unabashed action.

"He must be done lost his whole damn mind doing you like that! I say you let me call my cousins, you know, the twins? Girl, Larry and Barry'll put a whooping on him he'll never forget."

"Denise—"

"And don't worry. They'll be discreet."

"Uh, I take it Trevia told you about Lloyd?"

"Yeah, and I'm gonna pretend like I'm not hurt that *you* didn't call me."

"Denise—"

"It's okay. I guess it's still fresh and everything. So, where you at?"

"In Virginia, remember? For the Neo Soul Fest."

"You're still there with all that's happened?"

"Well…yeah. What was I supposed to do, catch the first flight I could get back home and pop up at his place acting a fool?"

"Hell, yeah!"

"Look, I'm a lot of things, but I'm not dumb. He's been ignoring my calls. He blocked me on Facebook. He's done, and I damn sure ain't begging him to change his mind."

"So what are you gonna do?"

"I'm gonna stay here and do my job. Take pictures, get a feel for this event. What I always do."

"No, I mean what are you gonna do about Lloyd?"

I sighed as I appraised myself in the mirror. Denise had caught me on my way out to try and enjoy the third and final day of the festival. I had wanted to get there when the gates opened that morning, but this call thwarted that plan. "I'm gonna try not to think about him, and when I get home, I'm gonna try to get over him."

"Wow, if I had your attitude, I'd probably get into a lot less trouble."

"Girl, I'm thirty years old, and Lloyd is not the first man to disappoint me."

"But you were in love and engaged."

I rubbed a finger across my ring. "Apparently, his ass is *still* in love and engaged."

"Bastard."

"You know what upsets me more than anything? That I didn't see this coming. I really thought everything was good."

"I know. I'm so sorry. I swear I wanna ride up on him and kick his high-yellow ass right now!"

"Nah, it's okay. Look, I need to head out. I'll call you from the airport tomorrow."

"Okay, have fun."

"I will."

5

Greer

I stepped onto the elevator, relieved to find it empty. The conversation with Denise had forced me to face feelings I'd decided to bury at least until this trip was over. I wanted to leave the hurt and disappointment back home in Texas and deal with the fall-out later. But now everything weighed heavily on me. The fact that my man had unceremoniously dumped me hung before my face like a seven-foot, flashing neon sign.

I loved Lloyd. I really did. It wasn't a devastating, Romeo and Juliet, "I'd die without you" type of love. But it was love—comfortable, reliable, "I can count on you," love. And he really wasn't that bad in bed, not as bad as I put it in that phone call. I mean, he wasn't that good, either. But I loved him, so I looked past it. After all, sex isn't everything.

I was so deep in thought that when I stepped out of the elevator and found myself walking face-first into a great-smelling, hard broad chest, I mumbled, "Excuse me," without looking up.

"Hey, I didn't know you were staying here, too. You disappeared on me after the show last night. We could've ridden back here together."

It was fine-chocolate-dreadlocks, AKA Derek. His thick lips were curved up in a disarming smile.

I shrugged and tried to calm my heart, which was beating like a jackhammer for some reason. Either he had startled me or he was turning me on. I was too messed up in the head to readily tell the difference. "I figured I'd bothered you enough," I said.

His wide smile morphed into a lopsided one. "Never that, Monique."

I started to give him my real name but actually liked the sound of Monique.

"Hey, you wanna wait a sec while I run up to my room? We can ride together," he offered.

I nodded. "Okay." Maybe being in his presence would take my mind off of my shit show of a life.

I stood close to the elevator bank and took out my phone, having decided to check my email. I had a couple of business-related messages...and one from Lloyd. Against my better judgment, I opened it.

My eyes swept over the words three times before I shoved my phone into my little purse: *I'm sorry.*

*****

I purposely bypassed the liquor vendors after we made it to the park. Yes, I was bummed and supremely pissed, and hell, hurt to be damned, but I wasn't going to spend my last day in Virginia, the day Maxwell was to perform, drunk. Plus, I wasn't going to turn into some damn alcoholic over Lloyd's ass, because if he could do this to me, he definitely wasn't worth me ruining my life over. I had already humiliated myself by semi-drunk dialing him. That was as low as I was willing to let this situation take me.

I wanted to be aware, maybe even hyperaware, of my surroundings. I wanted to absorb the sounds and sensations and tastes. I wanted my entire body to experience the sights and reverberations. I wanted my heart to feel the music instead of the absence of Lloyd.

Derek never left my side, and I appreciated him for that since I was a total and complete bitch to him before. We perused the vendors, grabbed a bite to eat, and then found a spot on the grass to enjoy the music together. We shared some benign conversation about the food, the people, and the music. Nothing heavy or personal. He didn't tell me his last name. Shoot, I wasn't even sure if Derek was his real name, and I was fine with that since he didn't know any of my actual names.

When Maxwell hit the stage, he snatched our attention away from each other and everything else, but I did glance at Derek a few times, mused to myself about how handsome he was, how gorgeous his deep brown skin and eyes were, how nice and muscular his arms were, how good he smelled, how long his legs were, how dazzling his smile was. And before I knew it, a heat began to travel over my body. I chalked it up to some sort of rebound horniness, or maybe it was the music, or the sensuality that seemed to crowd the atmosphere like atoms in a molecule. But one thing was for sure, I wanted me some Derek.

To try to cool myself down, I stood and danced to the music. He followed me to his feet, pumping his fist in the air to *Ascension* while singing along in a key that wasn't even in the same universe as

Maxwell's. My strategy was working pretty well until *Fortunate*.

As soon as Maxwell began belting out the falsetto intro, Derek grabbed my hand and shouted, "Aw, yeah! This is my shit!"

I giggled as he pulled me to him and led me in a slow dance right there on the grass. I leaned into him, because something about being in his long arms just felt...right. *Very* right. Right and good. Extremely good.

Maybe *too* good.

I closed my eyes as we danced and thanked the heavens he didn't try to sing along with the song.

As Maxwell continued to serenade some unknown woman about the fortuitousness of him having found her, Derek pulled me closer, leaned down and gently nuzzled my neck. I felt the bulge in front of him as he pressed his body against mine, and my body temperature shot up. My core pulsated, and there was a fluttering in my stomach. There was something so insanely intimate about the way Derek moved...something very nearly obscene. Sure, he had excellent rhythm, but there was something else, a magnetism I could neither explain nor deny, and it made me want to climb him like a tree. From the moment I first laid eyes on him I was drawn to him, despite the attitude I'd given him. I couldn't deny that.

The music, the crowd, *him*—it all enveloped me and surged through me like electricity. It was as if for a brief moment, we all became one. There was a naked purity in that feeling, the feeling of being exposed but protected at the same time. As if we all held a mutual secret that only the people present would ever know.

I looked up at him and slid my hands from his firm chest to his face, caressed his cheeks. He stared down at me; the smile that had become familiar to me was gone and a look that threatened to burn my flesh held its place. Our eyes locked and remained connected until a burst of applause sliced through our shared trance and reminded us where we were, that we were not alone, and that in truth, we didn't really know each other. I stepped out of his embrace feeling jaded, even a tad bit inebriated, as I reclaimed my seat on the grass. Derek sat beside me and grasped my hand in his as my heart thundered in my chest.

6

Greer

Derek left the festival before I did, as he had an early flight out the next morning. I decided to stay until the end to get some more pictures for my blog, but wished I'd left when he did. With him gone, I lost my focus on the concert. The music I'd felt such a connection to earlier faded into the background. The thrill of being in the midst of the crowd dissipated. The electric current surrounding me and coursing through me disappeared. I stood there as the baseline continued to thunder from the speakers and Maxwell crooned with expected precision. The people around me swayed to the music, but nothing felt the same in his absence. Time was marching on while I felt painfully stagnant. So moments later, I navigated a path through the crowd of melanated bodies and made my exit.

As I stepped out of the Uber, which was a downgrade from the Escalade I rode in with Derek, I sighed. I had spent the ride back to the hotel wiggling in the backseat of the car with my legs tightly clamped shut when what I really should've been doing was fanning my private parts, because my mind was laser-focused on Derek and how it felt to be in his arms. How that bulge felt against my body. How his eyes had seared into mine.

I was still hot and very bothered as I attempted to coolly stroll through the lobby to the elevator. I made the ride to the tenth floor alone, but Derek was still in my thoughts. I wondered how his hands would feel on my bare skin, gripping my naked butt. Or how his lips would feel on mine. Or how his tongue would feel—

The doors slid open and I exited the elevator with sagging shoulders and downcast eyes. Looked up a second later and from the sign on the wall, realized I had gotten off on the sixth floor, not the tenth. I turned and hit the up button on the elevator, now both horny and frustrated. The sooner I got to my room, the sooner I could take care of my frustrations myself, because there was no way I was going to be able to sleep through the throbbing between my legs.

The elevator opened with a ding and there he was, holding a key card in one hand and a candy bar in the other. He appeared just as surprised as I was as he stared at me before stepping out of the elevator and standing in front of me. My eyes never left him as the doors slid closed. There stood the remedy for an ache that was close to making me overheat. The scratch to a humongous itch. Reason fled my mind. Common sense was long gone. All I saw was him. All I felt was a need so deep and so great it was completely foreign to me. The magnetic pull of the man before me was nearly impossible to resist.

After standing in silence for a full minute with his eyes fastened to mine, he said, "I'm in 620."

I merely nodded, and when he turned to leave, I followed him, watching his perfect ass in jeans every pace of the path to his room. He unlocked the door and ushered me in without speaking a word.

I leaned against the wall and perused the room with my eyes, settling them on the neatly-made double beds. "You expecting anyone? A roommate?"

He shook his head as he dropped the key card and candy on the desk. "No."

"That's good."

"Monique—"

I moved closer to him. "Let's not beat around the bush. We know what we're here for. I know what you want, because I felt it when we danced, and I'm sure you know I want the same thing. We're both adults here, so my only question is: do you have protection, Derek?"

He smiled. "Being an adult... hell yes I do," he said huskily.

"That's good, too."

I reached up and placed my lips on his. When he wrapped his arms around me and swiftly pulled my body close to him, I dropped my little clutch on the floor and snaked my arms around his waist, parting my lips a bit, an invitation he accepted my dipping his tongue into my mouth. I moaned as his tongue found mine, moaned louder when his big hands found my round ass and squeezed. I followed his lead to one of the beds and didn't resist when he eased me onto it, our mouths still connected. My sex was vibrating unbearably as I lay back onto the mattress. He broke our connection for a moment, peering down at me. Through labored breaths, he whispered, "Damn..."

He must've been feeling what I was feeling, an inexplicable level of heat and passion, because he had echoed my thoughts with that one word. He placed his hand under my short skirt, his fingers sliding into my panties to my sex, stroking me. I gasped softly and arched my back, gazed up at him through intoxicated eyes and watched as he licked his lips. His mouth found mine again as his fingers continued to play a tune that threatened to send me over the edge.

"Aw, baby…" he murmured against my mouth.

He continued his torture for several minutes before I said, "Please…"

Burying his face in my neck, he suckled on my heated flesh. "Please, what?" He lifted his head and looked into my eyes. "What do you want me to do?"

"You know what," I whispered.

He slowly dragged his hand away from my sex. "You're ready for me?"

I nodded. "Yes."

He pulled my bikini top up to expose my breasts, gently tugged on an erect nipple, and said, "No, I don't think you are."

I closed my eyes as he devoured first the right, then the left breast. "I am. *Please…*" I repeated.

His mouth found mine again and our tongues danced for several minutes before he pulled away and said, "I think you might be ready now. Are you?"

"I'm more than ready."

As I watched him undress and sheath himself, I sat up to remove my soaked panties.

"Leave them on," he commanded.

Shit, okay, I thought. But rather than speak, I nodded and lay back on the bed, ready, willing, and able to give him all I had to offer. Especially now that I'd seen what *he* had to offer. Daaaaaaaaamn.

"Turn over."

I complied without hesitation. I wanted, no, *needed* this man inside of me. If I had to follow a few orders for it to happen, so be it.

I was on my knees, impatiently waiting, when I felt him climb in bed behind me. When he pressed himself against me, and without entering me, began to slowly grind against my butt, I almost lost it. Nothing in my life had ever felt so good. There was something about feeling him against me and knowing what was to come, knowing that as good as this felt, something even better was about to happen. I closed my eyes and moaned loudly. I was literally aching for this man. He rubbed himself against me for several seconds before I felt him slide my panties to the side and gently enter me. I grasped the sheets, released a groan as the length of his shaft slowly entered and exited my body.

"Monique..." he said as he glided inside of me again.

I offered him full access to my essence as I buried my face in the sheets and pressed my arms onto the bed, while keeping my hips raised and pushing my behind toward him. His hand felt warm as he placed it on the small of my back and plunged in and out of my moist center with increased ferocity, his other hand clutching my hip.

"Derek!" I screamed, as he filled me over and over again. Tears pooled in my eyes as we rode the waves of passion. He felt so good inside of me, better than I'd anticipated. He sexed me with rhythm and expertise, his naked body dripping beads of sweat onto mine.

"Yeah, baby?" he replied breathily.

"You. Feel. So. Good."

He continued thrusting, leaned forward, dipped his tongue in my ear, and whispered, "You feel better than good, baby."

I closed my eyes and listened to the sounds of our bodies mating, our ragged breathing, inhaled the thick scent of our sex in the air. I wished this moment would last forever—our bodies fitted together like lock and key, our senses heightened, our passions fully fulfilled. But climax was inevitable, and I wanted to feel the expected explosion almost as badly as I wanted to postpone it.

When we finally reached the peak together, I screamed, "Ooooh, shit! Derek!"

As he collapsed onto my back, he said, "Yeah, baby?"

7

Derek

The room was just as it was when we both fell asleep—my clothes on the floor, her bikini top half off, her skirt pushed up around her waist, the covers in a pile at the foot of the bed. The glow of the muted TV provided the only light; the singular sound was her soft breathing as she slept with her head on my bare chest, but the sounds of her humming and moaning still echoed around me, making my body want more of what she'd given me. I craned my neck and looked down at her, thought about her pretty round brown eyes that were now closed, wanted to kiss her full lips and taste her tongue again. I gently caressed the warm skin of her back. I was far from being a virgin, but what we'd shared was like nothing I'd ever felt before, and although I knew I needed to wake her up so I could get ready to leave, I didn't want to. What I wanted to do was bury my face—or myself—between her legs. I wanted some more of this mocha-skinned woman who was a full foot shorter than me with soft curves and braided hair.

If she wasn't wearing that ring, I might've canceled my plans for the week and convinced her to stay in Virginia with me. The thing was, I didn't know what her plans were or where she was from. I didn't even know her real name—first or last. What I did know was I was drawn to her like a damn moth to a flame. There was something broken inside of her, someone had hurt her recently, maybe the man who gave her the ring or the one on the phone. And I knew it was dangerous to get involved with someone who was dealing with whatever she might have been dealing with, but I didn't care. Hell, I was dealing with some shit, too. Some shit that should've had me running from this woman and any and all other women.

But there was just something about her.

I turned my head and glanced at the clock—4:00 AM. My flight left at five. I needed to leave, but instead, I grabbed my cell phone and noticed three missed calls from my brother, Brandon. I didn't bother listening to the voicemails he left. I knew he was probably pissed off, thinking I was going to make him and his wife miss their flight, so I texted him.

Me: *Hey, man. U 2 can head on out. I'm gonna catch a later flight.*

Brandon: *Damn, u couldn't let me know before now? I been calling ur rusty ass all morning!*

Me: *My bad. I overslept.*

Brandon: *I bet u did. Be careful. U know what happened the last time u "overslept."*

Me: *Whatever. I'll call u later.*

Brandon: *Alright.*

I eased the phone back onto the table and felt her stir.

"What time is it?" she asked through a yawn. "Did I spend the night?"

"Yeah, you did," I replied as I rubbed my thumb across her shoulder.

"Hmm, what time is it?" she repeated.

"A little after four."

"You need to leave? I can go back to my room. I need to start packing any—"

I flipped her onto her back and pinned her to the bed.

"Oh…so you *don't* want me to go?" she said with a slight grin.

I moved in and kissed her, and she gently bit my lip. I growled softly as she pushed me off of her onto my back, and straddled me. She pulled her bikini top completely off and my eyes took in the smoothness of the brown skin of her chest and neck. She leaned forward, dangling her breasts over me like a carrot in front of a horse. I reached up to touch them, but she swatted my hand away. "I thought you had an early flight," she said pointedly.

"I did." I lifted my head to kiss her again.

She straightened her posture, now just out of my reach, and shook her head. "Uh-uh, what happened?"

I sat up and faced her, pulled her closer to me and slid my hand between her legs. As I stroked her treasure, I said, "Change of plans."

8

Greer

I think maybe I lost my mind or something.

At the very least, I was pretty sure I could claim temporary insanity.

Why else would I have agreed to spend three more days in Virginia with a man who thought my name was Monique and whose last name he didn't bother to give me and I didn't bother to inquire about? Why else would I check out of my own room and move into his for those three days? Why did I share breakfast, lunch, and dinner with him every day and dessert with him between the sheets several times a day? Okay, maybe it was good-dick-itis. Because this man had mad, crazy, off-the-charts bedroom skills. Our sex was mind-blowing, explosive, and a laundry list of other superlatives that I could probably neither spell nor pronounce.

Good. Lord.

And he wasn't stingy with it, either. I lost count of how many times we made the bed in his room creak, how many times he made my insides turn into slush, how many times I shook and shuddered from the effects of his sex. I had never experienced anything like it before and to be totally honest, it was addictive.

Too addictive.

Now I understood why some women lost it over certain men. I didn't want to become that chick, but saw how easily it could happen. And then there was Lloyd, or rather my need to properly process the fact that there no longer was a Lloyd in my life, but how could I do that if I kept opening my legs for Derek, and lying underneath Derek, or climbing on top of Derek, or backing it up to Derek over and over and over and over and over and over and over again?

So when he asked if I wanted to extend our time together even further, I told him no. I had a life to get back to and a mind to find again. What we shared was wonderful, but it was superficial and unreal and futureless. We didn't know each other, hadn't even attempted to know each other. So six days after arriving in Virginia, I crept out of his room early that morning while he was in the shower, leaving behind a note thanking him for sharing his time and his room with me. I signed it *Monique.*

9

Greer

"Heifer, where have you been?!" greeted Trevia as soon as I stepped over the threshold into my apartment in Dallas. She was perched on a chair she'd evidently pulled from my kitchen into my living room.

Denise, who was sprawled out on my couch, interjected, "Probably off screwing some strange man. Shoot, that's what I would do if I were her."

"I'm taking my keys back. Y'all are abusing that privilege," I said as I walked through the living room to my bedroom, where I sat on the side of my bed and pulled my shoes off.

"We were checking on your house like you asked. You could have at least been courteous enough to call and tell us you were staying longer," Trevia said, as she and Denise followed me into my room.

"I texted you."

"A text is not a call," Denise offered.

I rolled my eyes. "I'm sorry, Wardens Trevia and Denise, that I did not call you two. We good now? Why aren't y'all at work?"

"It's seven in the evening. We're off," Trevia offered.

"Oh," I said. "Right."

Denise stood next to my dresser and stared at me as Trevia plopped down on the bed beside me.

"I didn't get you two any souvenirs this time. Sorry."

"What's his name?" Denise asked.

Trevia was now staring at me, too.

"Whose name?" I asked, trying not to smile.

Trevia hopped up and shouted, "You slept with some random guy in Virginia?! You?!"

"What do you mean *you*?" I asked, feeling a little offended. I wasn't a prude, was I?

"I'm just saying, you've never been the sex-without-a-relationship type. That's all."

"I never said I had sex with anyone, Trevia."

"But you did, and it was good. I can tell," Denise said with a grin on her face. "Details, please. I need to know who's got you glowing like that. Whoever he is had a magic touch that Lloyd definitely does not possess, because in all the time you two were together, I never saw you look like this or walk like you walked into this place a minute ago."

I hated she'd brought him up. I hadn't thought about him in days. "How was I walking, 'Nise?"

"Like someone put it on you!"

I smiled and gave them both a sly look. "That's probably because someone did…"

"Aw, snap! Do tell!" Trevia said with wide eyes.

"Well…"

I told them the truth—that we'd met at the festival, kept running into each other, and spent time together.

"He was really fine, huh?" Denise asked.

"Finer than fine," I replied.

"I know you took a picture of him," Trevia said.

"Um, actually I didn't."

"You're gonna keep in touch, see where things go?" Trevia asked.

"No, we didn't exchange information. I kind of wanted to leave what we shared in Virginia, you know?"

"Nope, because I would've gotten his number, address, social security number, blood type—"

"Denise!" Trevia and I screamed in unison.

"I'm just saying. That sounds like some kind of man."

"Yeah, he was."

They stayed for another thirty minutes before leaving. After locking the door behind them, I dug my cell phone out of my purse and scrolled to a picture I'd taken of Derek while he ate breakfast in our hotel room one morning. He was shirtless, and the sunlight from the window was hitting him just right. I sighed and fell onto my bed thinking about what we did after breakfast that morning.

10

Derek

"I bought a cat and named it Bitch Mode," my brother said.

I looked up from my steak and frowned. "What?"

"So you heard that? I was just checking, because I'm pretty sure you didn't hear anything else I've said during this entire conversation."

"I…I'm sorry, man."

"*You* invited *me* to lunch, remember? A supposed business lunch where we were supposed to discuss business, *our* business. You know, the little company our folks left us? But so far all you've done is stare at that sirloin and ignore me. The hell is wrong with you, Derek? Is it that chick from Virginia?"

"I don't think she's from Virginia," I said.

"You don't think? Come on, man…how can you be this messed up over a woman when you don't even know where she lives?"

I picked up the knife and fork and cut into the steak—medium well to perfection. "Shit, Brandon, I don't know. Hey, what were you saying about the Hofstra account?"

"Don't change the subject now. You need to call that woman and talk to her or something. Schedule a booty call. Do something so you can get back to normal. We've got a company to run and you can't do it if you're stuck in some sprung catatonic state."

I took a bite of my steak. "I'm not sprung."

"The hell you're not. I know sprung when I see it. Being sprung is what got me married. *I know sprung.*"

I chuckled. "Yeah, you've been sprung forever, man. Forever."

"With good reason. Believe me. So, you gonna call her?"

I cleared my throat and leaned back in my chair. "I can't. I don't have her number."

"What?! You spent damn near a week with her and you didn't get her number?"

"I actually spent three days and four nights with her. It took me the three days before that just to get with her."

He stared at me.

"Uh...we kind of didn't share much personal information. It was fun at first, you know? I liked the freedom of it, and I figured it was best with my current situation." I didn't bother to tell him I had planned to exchange information with her before we parted ways but she ducked out on me before we could. I was still a little pissed and maybe even a little hurt about that, because while I could admit I might've been sprung, I was positive that she was, too.

"You shouldn't be in that situation and you know it. I told you—"

"I know what you told me about her, but do you have to rub it in? I'm working on fixing it."

"You keep saying that, but nothing has changed, little bro. Hey, I'm just looking out for you like I always have."

"I know, I know. I thought I had a handle on things, but..."

"You didn't count on getting sprung in the meantime, huh?"

"No, I didn't."

"What are you gonna do about it, the Virginia woman situation, I mean?"

"Nothing. I'm going to concentrate on work and straightening up the mess I made."

"That's it?"

"What else can I do?"

"Try to find her."

I shook my head. "I don't think she wants to be found, and I ain't into forcing myself on no one. Never have, and never will."

"What makes you say she doesn't want to be found?"

"Just a feeling. Let's just drop it and talk business. I'm listening."

11

Greer

...Overall, my experience at the Neo Soul Festival was wonderful. The variety of food vendors was excellent. If you go next year, be sure to check out Andress's Caribbean Delights. Their jerk chicken was nothing short of divine. If you have a sweet tooth, try the fried dough at Margaret's. And for libations, try Jimmy's.

My favorite product vendor was Katrina's Scentsations, which carried everything from scented natural soaps to soy candles. I'd also like to mention Grass Roots, a vendor that sold African print women's clothing. I copped a gorgeous skirt from them (See picture below). I hope these vendors return next year, but if not, I'm told they are all local businesses, so if you happen to visit Cromer, Virginia, be sure to give them your business.

All in all, I give the hotel a B+ and the festival itself an A.

Until next time, I'm Greer Kennedy,

Your Nubian Nomad.

As I finally ended my past-due blog post, I sat back and sighed, glanced at the ring I still wore for some crazy reason, and wished I could share the entire truth with my readers. It would've been nice if I could tell them my frame of mind, how I arrived in Virginia a happily engaged woman and how that changed in less than twenty-four hours after my arrival. Or how I chose to cope with an unexpected break-up by having anonymous sex with a strange guy who had to have majored in Putting It On A Woman 101 in college, graduated Summa Cum Laude, and then went on to obtain his Ph.D. and was now known as Dr. The Best Sex You'll Ever Have In Your Entire Life. All of that would've been scandalous and made me seem like a ho', but it would've made for a much more interesting post, because what I'd written sounded dry and uninteresting to *me*. I could only imagine how it would bore my readers to tears.

I was off my game, and it was all Lloyd's fault. My posts were usually filled with anecdotal humor. I was convinced that was what made my blog popular enough to attract great sponsors and draw tons of readers every month. But I found it hard to think of anything humorous to share with my readers, because my mind was in a my-fiancé-dumped-me-via-Facebook haze and I was sure it was because I didn't have any closure. It had been a week since I returned home, more than a week since the ball dropped and smashed my future, and I still didn't understand why what happened…happened. Lloyd had not called me to explain or offer a real apology, and I hadn't attempted to call or see him. Maybe I should've taken Denise's advice and rode up on him.

No, I wasn't going to do that. I wasn't going to pop up and act a fool over some man who obviously didn't want me.

But I needed—no—I *deserved* answers.

Yeah, after two years of a relationship, I deserved much more than a two-word email, and I was going to get it. I glanced at the time on my phone—7:30 PM. He'd be home from work by now if he was still the

Lloyd I knew and loved, a true creature of habit. Lloyd was steady, predictable. Or at least he was until he dumped me. I definitely wasn't expecting that.

I grabbed my keys and purse, looked down at my t-shirt and joggers, and shook my head. I wasn't going to confront the man looking like I was pining away for him even if I kind of, sort of was. I was going to look so good, he'd see me and instantly regret his actions. So I showered for the first time that day, sprayed on his favorite perfume, dressed in a black sleeveless jumpsuit and a pair of red stilettos, pulled my braids up into a top knot, applied mascara, eye-liner, and lip gloss, and left.

It was when I arrived at Lloyd's house that I got cold feet. I should've called Denise and had her ride with me.

I parked down the street a ways from his ranch-style home, a home I'd spent many nights in—and started having second thoughts. What if he spotted my loud-ass car sitting on the street and called the police or something since he obviously didn't want to be bothered with me? What if I knocked and he found out it was me at the door and ignored me? Or what if he opened the door and treated me like some stalker? What if he slammed it in my face? No, I couldn't take the chance of any of that happening. I'd already been humiliated enough since everyone we knew was aware of the fact that he was now engaged to another woman. And anyone who followed Lloyd on Facebook knew he was engaged to me one day and Tami the next. Yep, that was definitely enough humiliation.

Maybe I should've attempted to have a relationship with Dr. The

Best Sex You'll Ever Have In Your Entire Life. If I had, perhaps my stupid ass wouldn't have been sitting down the street from Lloyd's, staring at his car in his driveway feeling...well, dumb.

I gripped the key, ready to start my car and leave, when I saw him. Tall, handsome, used to be mine. He had walked out of the front door and stepped to the side. A second later, a woman walked out and grabbed his hand. A woman I'd never seen before.

Tami?

I watched Lloyd close the door and lock it. He wore the red oxford shirt I bought him for his birthday a couple of months earlier, because I thought his monochrome-wearing ass needed some color in his life. But at that moment, I wanted to snatch that bitch off his deceptive, two-timing ass, wrap one of the sleeves around his neck, and strangle him with it. He was also wearing slacks. Tami was wearing a blue swing dress. She was much shorter than him. She even looked to be shorter than my five-feet, three inches. From what I could see at that distance, she looked attractive enough—medium brown skin, shoulder-length hair styled in a bob, maybe a size eight to my size ten. I supposed they were heading out to celebrate something like making the Nubian Nomad look like a damn fool, or maybe they were just going out to dinner. Lloyd was always good for a dinner date.

He walked her to the passenger side of his BMW, which I had a good view of from my vantage point, and before opening the door for her, he kissed her. Then he placed his hand on her stomach, bent over, and kissed it, too.

She was pregnant?

12

Greer

I sat there for thirty minutes after he left before the shock and numbness wore off, then I climbed out of my car, walked to his house, and tried my key to his door to find the lock had been changed, but was that really a surprise? I stood there for a minute and noticed the mail slot on the door that had always been there, thought about the love notes I'd drop in there sometimes just so he'd have a little surprise when he made it home from work. I snatched the ring off of my finger, opened the mail slot, and tossed the ring inside where I heard it land on his hardwood floor. I hoped his ass stepped on it, had a little slip and fall, and broke his damn neck. What a total piece of shit!

I kind of hoped Tami wouldn't be the victim of a slip and fall at my hands since she was with child, but if she was, so be it. She shouldn't have gotten herself knocked up by my man.

When I got back to my place, I purged it of any evidence that Lloyd existed—ripped up pictures and cards, threw away gifts no matter how expensive they were. Got rid of his toothbrush and the two or three shirts and pairs of pants he'd left at my place. I deleted my Facebook page altogether rather than just change my relationship status. My main social media outlets for the blog were Instagram and Twitter, and as those were where the bulk of my followers were, I wasn't worried about having a Facebook page. I deleted any emails or text messages I'd ever received from him, finally called my parents and told them the engagement was off. I actually think they were glad they wouldn't have to come back to the states for the wedding since they spent all of their time traveling abroad. After I'd successfully deleted Lloyd Robinson from my life, I sat on my sofa and stared into space for a solid hour before calling Trevia.

"Hey, what's up?" she chirped into the phone.

My answer was to sob loudly into her ear.

"I'll be right there after I pick up Denise," she responded.

*****

"She's pregnant?!" Denise shouted after I brought her and Trevia up to speed on my little trip to Lloyd's.

I nodded. "Yeah, I can't believe this shit. I mean. How did I miss this?" I took a bite of the ice cream Trevia had brought with her.

Denise shoveled a piece of her mom's sweet potato pie into her mouth, and between bites said, "Because he had to be experienced at cheating."

"But I'm not dumb. I know the signs from my other relationships and from watching you two. Hell, my daddy was a cheater back in the day. I knew better than to get caught off guard like this. I trusted him. Maybe I should've just moved in with him when he asked me to."

Trevia shook her head. "Don't do that. It's not your fault. But, just out of curiosity, why didn't you move in with him?"

I shrugged and placed my bowl on the coffee table. "I like having my own space, and Lloyd is so particular about his stuff. You have to take your shoes off at the door. Stuff like that."

"Then how in the hell were you going to be married to him?"

"I figured once we married and combined our lives and our stuff we could come to some type of compromise. That's what you do when you love someone."

Denise nodded but didn't respond. Neither did Trevia.

"Y'all think I was stupid, don't you? We were too mismatched, weren't we? He hated that I traveled so much even though it's my job. Said he didn't get why I like traveling alone. He didn't like most of my clothes, thought my look was too bohemian, hated my furniture, especially this yellow-ass couch. We were incompatible, and it took him dumping me without telling me he was dumping me for me to realize it. Shit, I'm an idiot."

"No, you were in love. Believe me, I know how that can shut your damn brain down. It's like love and logical thinking can't coexist," Denise offered. "But I applaud you for not running up on him and his whore and beating their asses."

"Hear, hear!" Trevia said, lifting her slice of pie in the air like a wine glass. "Nasty trick needs to be throat punched!"

"Y'all know that's not my style."

"Well, it's *my* style," Denise said, flipping her jet-black weave over her shoulder. "That along with slashing tires and taking a bat to a windshield. Lloyd is lucky he messed over you and not me!"

"I know that's right!" Trevia chimed in.

I was obviously the voice of reason among the three of us, always had been, but even I had to admit the thought of wrecking Lloyd's shit sounded therapeutic. "Don't tempt me," I said.

"I wonder what his new fiancée does for a living since he had a problem with you traveling so much," Denise said.

"She's definitely not a beautician," I mused. "Because that bob was tragic."

Denise fell back onto the sofa and cackled loudly.

"Nope, she's a teacher," Trevia informed us.

"How do you know that?" I asked.

"I told you I checked out Lloyd's page using my sister's account. His page led me to *her* page, where I found out her full name. She doesn't share much publicly, but there was one photo that was linked to her Instagram account which *is* public." She grabbed her phone from the coffee table, swiped at it a few times, and then handed it to me. "See, Tami Fletcher. Kindergarten teacher at Belk Elementary."

I held the phone and stared at the pictures. Her alone. Her with her friends. Her with her sorors holding up some hand sign. And the most recent picture was of her hand, showcasing her ring. "Bastard bought us the same ring! What did he do? Get a multi-purchase discount?"

"Yeah, I saw that," Detective Trevia said.

Denise snatched the phone from me. "That sure in the hell is the same ring! What is wrong with him? Son-of-a-bitch!"

I shook my head and stood from the sofa, walked over to the window that overlooked my apartment complex's pool. "She looks nice. Maybe she didn't know about us."

"She knew," Trevia said.

I glanced at her. "Now how in the world would you know that?"

"Look at her page. There's no mention of Lloyd anywhere, no pictures of him either. She didn't even mention his name under the picture of the ring. And all of her friends are under there commenting about how they didn't know she was seeing anyone. She knew he was taken."

I shook my head, amazed at her investigative skills. "You should've been a PI or something."

She laughed. "Oh, no. I love making clothes. That's my thing. Being with Wesley, I have to be able to follow clues. His ass is as slick as they come. That's how I acquired these skills."

I reserved any comments I might have had about her man for later, and besides, she knew how I felt about Wesley Anderson. Sure, he was attractive, sexy even, but his job as an exotic dancer exposed him to the one thing he couldn't resist—women, and a lot of them. For the life of me I never understood why she stayed with him all these years. Trevia was tall and slim with flawless mahogany skin and exotic-looking almond eyes, and she was a beast with a sewing machine. She owned her own boutique and made good money. She didn't need Wesley's trifling ass.

"I've been through some stuff, too," Denise said, "but I don't have your skills, Trevia. You need to teach me your ways for the next man I get."

"Why, so you can torture the man with the intel you gather?" Trevia asked.

"Yep," Denise confirmed through a belch.

We all laughed.

Denise rubbed her stomach and said, "Greer, your ass needs to stop laughing and come eat this pie I stole from my mother's freezer. I think it's one of the ones she cooked earlier this summer and was saving for the holidays. She's gonna have a fit when she finds out it's missing, and even with all the folks that come in and out of that house, she's gonna know it was me."

I walked back over to the sofa and reclaimed my seat between my friends. "You didn't have to steal your mama's pie, 'Nise, although I do appreciate it. Can't nobody make a pie like Ms. Jenny. Patti ain't got nothing on her!"

"Yeah, my mama's mean as a snake, but she can cook her ass off. It's the only good thing about living there. I'll be glad when I can move out! I miss having my own place."

"You making any progress towards moving?" I asked.

"Still trying to pay off some stuff and fix my credit so I can get a decent place. The problem is, once I think I've got a handle on things, another account or credit card in my damn name pops up from out of nowhere that I knew nothing about! If my credit was five years ago what it is now, I wouldn't have gotten my job at the bank. Hell, I'm a loan officer who couldn't get a loan at my own bank if my life depended on it. Kevin Buhari really screwed up my finances and my life. I will never get married again. Worst decision I ever made."

I looked over at my friend who was the shortest of the three of us at five feet even. I always thought she was so pretty with her honey brown skin and round face. She was about a size twenty with curves in all the right places, what most men would term thick. "He had us all fooled, 'Nise," I said.

"Yeah, he seemed so nice. Who knew he'd wreck your credit, empty your bank accounts, and bail?" Trevia offered.

"I know, right? But I got his ass!" Denise said, hopping up from the couch and swinging an imaginary bat.

I doubled over in laughter. "Girl, I have never seen a car that jacked up! And when you went after him? I've never seen a man run that fast in my life!"

Trevia was laughing so hard, she slid from the couch to the floor. "Yeah, there me and Greer were trying to hold you back, and Usain Bolt couldn't have caught him if he tried!"

Denise laughed and said, "Enough about Kevin's sorry behind. No, enough about sorry men, period! We got pie and ice cream to eat, and you got Netflix. I'm trying to watch Luke Cage's fine ass."

13

Derek

I stood at the door of my house and almost wondered if I should knock. Better yet, I thought I should just leave, but I needed to check on the place since I hadn't stepped foot in it in more than two weeks. I also needed to pick up some of my things. So I took a deep breath and unlocked the door, stepped inside, and yelled, "Anyone here?"

I was relieved when I was met with complete silence. I picked up the stack of mail from the table in the entryway and rifled through it as I made my way up the stairs to my bedroom. Everything was undisturbed and since I was alone, I decided to take a quick shower in my own home and change before heading back out. After all, I'd had the shower custom built to my specifications, including the ceiling-mount rain head with multiple spray options. As soon as I stepped into the spacious stall and felt the warm water rain down on me, I remembered why I loved my place so much. I'd really missed it.

Twenty minutes later, I stepped out of the shower and toweled off, grabbed a robe and put it on just in case. Good thing I did, because there was a surprise waiting for me when I entered my bedroom.

"I didn't know you were coming home today," Sasha said from her seat on the side of my bed. I hated the way she made it sound like we were sharing a home or something.

I walked to the closet and pulled out a pair of jeans and a t-shirt. "I needed to pick up some things."

"Oh...you wanna stay for dinner? I could hook something up real quick for you. I know you're in a hurry to leave. You always are."

Was she trying to sound pitiful, like this entire situation was my fault? "No, I'm good. I'll grab something after I leave." I dug through my drawer for some underwear.

"Fast food? You hate fast food. Don't be like that, let me fix you something. It's the least I could do."

I squeezed my eyes shut for a second and sighed. "No...thank you."

"Derek, are you ever going to stop being mad at me?"

My back was to her, but I could hear the quiver in her voice. "I'm not mad, I'm just...you know what? I'm doing the best I can under the circumstances."

"You ran away from your own house! I hear you've been sleeping in your office like some homeless man! How is that doing your best? Why won't you just stay here?"

I turned around to find that she had left the bed and was standing only a few inches away from me. "Because I don't want to be around you."

I could see the tears in her eyes. "You don't have to be so cruel."

"Cruel? I opened my home up to you when you had nowhere to go! That's cruel?"

"No...you know what I mean." She rubbed her hand over her bulging stomach, which seemed to have doubled in size since I saw her last.

"You're the one who's being cruel about that, not me."

"No I'm not!"

"Then agree to the test. Let's find out for sure whose baby that is."

"It's yours, Derek. I already told you that."

"Sasha, I'm not some careless kid. I'm careful, very careful, *always*. I don't believe that's my baby."

"Then why am I here? Why are you letting me stay here?"

"Because, one: you needed a place to stay. I wasn't going to let you be homeless whether that's my baby or not. Two, I did have sex with you so there's a chance, a slim one, but a chance the baby is mine. But I want the test done. I'll pay for it. I need to know for sure if that's my baby."

"I'm telling you it is! And I'm not getting some test that could hurt our child!"

"You know it doesn't have to be invasive. You just like this, don't you? You like being able to hold this over my head. We're over, Sasha. OVER. We were over before you moved in here. We were over before you popped up pregnant. Hell, you could be pregnant with octuplets by me and we'd *still* be over."

"Why?" she whined. "Why can't we try to make it work again? We were so good together…"

"Because you cheated on me, or did you forget that?"

"No, I didn't cheat! Not really. I mean, it's not like I cared about him. It just happened."

"Yeah, as if it makes it better that you busted it open for some random dude you didn't care about. I want the test done. And you need to find you a place. Didn't you have homeowner's insurance?"

"Yes. I told you, I'm waiting for the insurance company to pay me."

"You probably burned your own damn house down just to get my sympathy. Gonna get your ass arrested for arson."

Her mouth dropped open. "I can't believe you would say something like that! I lost everything in that fire! You think I would do that on purpose? You think I wanna be here at your mercy?"

"As a matter of fact, I do."

She shook her head. "Something is going on. You've never been this mean to me before. Is there someone else?"

"Someone else? There would have to be an *us* for that term to apply, Sasha. Look, I need to get dressed, so I'm gonna need for you to leave my room."

"It's not like I've never seen it before."

"Damn it, go!"

She dropped her eyes and her lip trembled as she scurried out of the room.

I locked the door behind her, sat on my bed, and wondered how I'd gotten myself into this mess.

14

Greer

Things were getting back to normal for me and when I wasn't planning my next trip, I was working hard to secure some affiliate deals, sell ads, and form partnerships. My big project was trying to strike a deal with an airline company to partner with my blog.

My plan, as I shared it with several companies, was for them to provide me with discounted airfare in exchange for virtually unlimited exposure to my readers via my reviews of their services, prominent and possibly permanent ad placement, and inclusion in my recommended companies if applicable, not to mention the possibility of their company being featured in any articles I wrote for other publications, which I did from time to time. In my correspondence with the companies, I informed them that my reader demographic—young, successful African Americans—would readily support any company that showed interest in servicing them. I argued that this demographic was an adventurous group who traveled often both for work and for play. I made several points that should've had these companies jumping at the chance to at least place an ad on my blog, if not provide me with the discounted airfare.

I contacted the companies via email and snail mail and had been turned down by every last one of them so far. I was still waiting to hear from three more companies, including the company Lloyd worked for, but things didn't look good as far as this little pet project of mine was going. It was frustrating that no one was even entertaining my idea. It wasn't like I wanted something for nothing. What I wanted was to create a mutually beneficial arrangement, and I would've thought these companies would be glad to diversify their marketing efforts. What better way to do that than to partner with an African American travel blogger with a huge following? Evidently, young African American dollars meant nothing to them.

I hit send on another email to another company then reclined in my chair and rubbed my tired eyes. I'd been staring at the computer for hours. Standing up from my desk, I stretched my pajama-clad body and shuffled to the kitchen to grab a bite. I had a bad habit of plowing through work without eating. It was three in the afternoon and I hadn't had a bite to eat all day.

I was almost done with my peanut butter and honey sandwich when my mother called. "Hello?" I answered, and gulped down some almond milk.

"Hey, sweetie! How are you? Things okay?" That was her way of asking without asking about how I was coping with my broken engagement.

"I'm fine. Working. How are you guys?"

"Good. Dad says hi."

"Tell him I said hey. Where are you two this month?" I asked, as I hopped up from my sofa and sat at my desk again. Since my father retired from his government job, my parents had been using their savings and his retirement to travel the world. They hadn't set foot on US soil in three years and had no intentions of returning any time soon. They were living it up and they deserved it.

"Paris. You should come visit."

"Hmm, maybe I will." I tapped the mouse pad and saw that I'd received an email from Adventure Airlines. "Hey, Ma, let me call you back."

"Okay, honey."

I laid my phone on the desk and opened the email, fully expecting another rejection, and that was exactly what I received. What I didn't expect was for the email and very nice letter to come from Lloyd Robinson.

*****

Denise sat on my living room floor staring in awe at my laptop. "When did Lloyd get to be VP of Marketing? I thought he worked in corporate compliance or something like that."

"He did. Guess he has a new position," I said.

"Bastard. I knew we should've rode up on his ass."

I kicked my legs up on the sofa and rolled over on my side. "He's not worth the trouble. Hey, where's Trevia? She never misses our spa night."

"When I went by her place to scoop her up, she said she'd be over later. I think she and Wesley were into it or something."

"I don't know why she stays with him."

"Because he's fine with a huge penis. Are you forgetting that we all met him at the same strip show? Trevia just happened to decide to take him home."

"I know. I can't believe it's lasted three years."

"It hasn't, not really. They've just spent three years breaking up and making up. She knows he's not going to act right. I think she likes the drama."

I shrugged. "Maybe. I just wish she'd leave his sorry ass. She's too good for him."

Denise's phone chimed and she said, "Speak of the devil. She just texted me. Says she can't make it."

I shook my head. "Did she tell you about what happened last week?"

Denise placed my computer on the coffee table and turned to face me. "No, what?"

"When she got home from work last Wednesday, there was a woman beating on her front door screaming that Mr. Bigg Blakk burned her."

Denise's mouth fell open. "What?! You mean—"

"Wesley supposedly gave her a VD. Trevia said she was livid. You know she stays in a nice neighborhood. The neighbors were outside and everything. When she tried to calm the woman down, the woman swung at her. Then Wesley finally came outside and pulled the woman off of Trevia. *Then* someone called the police. It was a hot mess."

"Damn! And they're still together? The hell is wrong with Trevia?

He probably gave her something, too!"

"I just don't know what her deal is."

"I'd break out my bat and wreck his shit for her, but it won't help. She'd probably just pay for it to get fixed. Girl, I don't want no parts of a penis like his. It's like acid to brain cells."

"Right? Good penis will make you lose your mind."

We both laughed.

Denise gave me a sly look. "Hey, speaking of good penis…"

"Girl, I can't lie. I kind of wish I could get in touch with Virginia Derek. Because honey, he was the bomb!"

"Woo, be careful. I ain't got a man right now and I broke my vibrator."

"Damn, you broke it? How much were you using it?"

"Shut up."

I snickered as she snatched my laptop back down to her lap.

"You break it, you pay for it…just like that vibrator," I said with a smirk.

"Kiss my ass. Hey, you got an email from Sable Jets."

"Who? What's Sable Jets?"

"How would I know?"

"Open it and read it."

"Okay."

Denise had been reading silently for several minutes before I said, "What's it say?"

"That they are a private jet charter company and they want to partner with your blog."

"What?!" I shrieked.

"And get this, the partnership would include them providing you with air travel...for FREE!"

"A private jet? A *free* private jet?" I sat up, yanked the computer from her, and quickly read the email. "I can't believe this."

Denise plopped down on the sofa next to me. "Believe it, sis. And...feel free to hook me up with a ride or two."

I rolled my eyes as I began typing my response to Sable Jets.

15

Greer

My meeting with Millie Graham, the head of marketing at Sable Jets, was at the offices of its parent company, Sable Inc., and so, a week after receiving that email from her, I happily found myself in downtown Houston in the lobby of a huge, towering building. I boarded the elevator and rode it to the ninth floor along with several other people. Some already looked harried at ten in the morning, others just looked tired. That was what I loved most about my career; since I was my own boss, I set my own schedule and worked at my own pace which served to alleviate stress for the most part. But this meeting and what it could do for my career was pulling at my nerves. I was so anxious that I almost didn't get off at the right floor. My meeting was at 10:30 AM, but I didn't want to take even a slim chance of being late.

When I arrived at Sable Inc., I was greeted by a receptionist whose warm smile eased my tension a bit. She offered me a seat across from her huge glass-top desk and told me Millie would be with me shortly, offered me some coffee which I readily accepted. Big mistake. The caffeine heightened my anxiety. By the time a petite, mid-twentyish woman wearing a gorgeous black pantsuit approached me and introduced herself as Millie Graham, I was ready to climb the walls.

"Greer Kennedy," I managed to say as I accepted her outstretched hand.

She pushed a tuft of her natural hair behind her ear, adjusted her thin, rectangular eyeglasses, and clapped her hands together. "Well, please follow me. I cannot tell you how excited I am about this meeting. Like I told you on the phone, I am a huge fan of your blog!"

I followed her along a carpeted pathway that separated a maze of cubicles from a row of offices, and finally into a huge boardroom that held a long glass table surrounded by at least twenty sleek, black leather chairs. The table held four black folders and four glasses of water.

I glanced at the lovely abstract art on the wall, and asked, "Um, where should I sit?"

"Anywhere there's a folder except the spot at the head of the table. That's reserved for the CEO, Mr. Hill."

"One of the Hill brothers?" I asked. I remembered seeing something in the Sable Inc. information she sent me about the company being run by the Hill brothers.

"Yes. When he found out about our meeting this morning, he insisted on sitting in. It's kind of strange, because he usually doesn't deal with any business at this level. Bigger fish to fry, you know? I guess he's just as excited as I am about the potential of this deal."

I nodded and took a seat opposite the one Millie had claimed. My nervousness expanded at the prospect of this big-wig being present. I looked down at my attire and decided my skirt was too short. *I look like I'm trying to sell my ass instead of my blog,* I thought.

A few seconds later, a man walked in and took a seat on the opposite side of the table from me, right next to Millie.

"Ms. Kennedy, this is Derek Scott, my assistant."

Hearing the name Derek made goosebumps rise along my arms. As the man stood and walked around the table to shake my hand, I smiled while trying to wipe images of a naked Virginia Derek from my mind. Once this other Derek was seated again, I took a sip of water and then played with the edges of the glossy black folder before me with the *Sable Jets* logo etched on the cover in gold. I closed my eyes, took a deep breath, and when I heard the door open with a soft whoosh, opened my eyes to see Virginia Derek AKA Dr. The Best Sex You'll Ever Have In Your Entire Life AKA fine-chocolate-dreadlocks enter the room and take a seat at the head of the table.

16

Greer

If my entire body had not been paralyzed, including my face, my mouth might have dropped open, or perhaps I would've hopped up and sprinted out of the room. But as it was, I sat there and stared at him in his navy blue suit that fit him so well you would've thought his fine ass was born in it. His dreads hung loosely, just past his shoulders. He was clean shaven in Virginia but was now sporting a neat goatee and mustache. His dark eyes were glued to me. The region between my legs instantly turned to mush.

Shit! I thought. *Shit, shit, double shit!*

My four-night-stand is the CEO?

Shit, damn, hell! I can hang this deal up. Pretty sure he doesn't do business with hoes, especially not with hoes who leave him in hotel rooms.

"Thanks for joining us, Mr. Hill. This is Greer Kennedy. Ms. Kennedy, this is Sable Inc.'s CEO, Mr. Derek Hill," Millie said.

When he rose, I rose, but stood still as he took the few steps to shake my hand. He smiled, his eyes on my lips. "It's truly a pleasure, Ms. Kennedy."

I opened my mouth, only managed to croak out, "T-thank you."

He gave me a little nod, and stroked the inside of my hand with his thumb before releasing it. I fell into my seat and mechanically opened the folder when instructed to by Millie. I tried to at least act like I was listening to her, but didn't hear a word she said. My eyes had a mind of their own as they kept darting to Derek, who evidently stared at me the whole time with an expression on his face that had no place in a boardroom. It was a look that provoked some pretty explicit memories, and before I knew it, I had grabbed the folder and was fanning myself with it.

Millie stopped mid-sentence and asked, "Are you warm, Ms. Kennedy? I'm cold-natured so I'm bad about keeping rooms too warm."

Shit. I dropped the folder on the table. "No, I just...it's me. Um, continue, please."

She glanced at Derek who was still staring at me. "Okay..."

I started playing with my watch and then started tapping my foot. Finally, I interrupted Millie with, "I, this was a mistake. I'm sorry I wasted your time, but this isn't going to work. I'm really, really sorry."

Millie looked taken aback. "Well, I haven't even finished my presentation and—"

"Millie, can you give me and Ms. Kennedy the room?" Derek asked, addressing her but still looking at me.

"Sir?" she asked, confusion evident in her voice.

"Can you and Mr. Scott give us the room?"

She hesitated and then said, "Sure. Yes, sir."

They left, and Derek moved to a chair right beside mine.

My eyes reluctantly met his. "Did you-did you know who I was before I got here today?"

He nodded. "Yes, I did."

17

Derek

2 Hours Earlier…

The day started off so badly I was sure it would only get worse. I spent the night at a hotel, because Brandon had been on my case about how it looked for the CEO to be sleeping in his office, said it made me look either broke or crazy—not a good look at all for the company. I tried to argue that I didn't want to waste the money and explained that I actually liked sleeping in my office. The couch was really comfortable, there was a private bathroom in my office suite, and if I went home early enough in the morning hours, Sasha would sleep through my shower and I could dress and duck back out of my house undetected. I had it all figured out and it was working for me, but Brandon insisted I get a room or go home. I was so tired of arguing about it, I gave in, went ahead and got a room, because I damn sure wasn't spending an entire night under the same roof as Sasha's underhanded ass. There wasn't much I put past her, including raping me in my sleep.

So I got a room downtown, paid too damn much for a suite thinking it would feel more like home, and didn't get a wink of sleep because being in that hotel room reminded me of *her*.

Monique, if that was really her name.

I could smell her and feel her and well, my body reacted to all of that, making it difficult for me to get any rest. So I took care of my own needs and still couldn't get to sleep. When I don't get my proper rest, I can be an asshole. This time was no different. I was pissed off from the time I climbed out of bed to the second I walked into the office.

I had meetings, phone calls, and all kinds of other shit I didn't care to deal with as it was, so when Millie tapped on my door asking to see me, I damn near cut her head off.

"What?!" I yelled.

She actually physically jumped. "Um, I have that meeting with the travel blogger this morning..."

I looked up from my computer with raised brows. "And?"

"And you wanted to see the final proposal before I present it to her?" She didn't sound at all sure of that fact.

"Oh...right." I held out my hand.

She cautiously approached me and handed me a folder, then stood awkwardly by my desk.

"Have a seat," I offered, feeling a little sheepish.

She sat in front of my desk as I perused the proposal. A little of my irritation dissipated as I read it. Millie was smart to come up with this idea of partnering with a blogger, and everything looked to be in order until I flipped to the back of the folder and saw a sheet of paper that looked to be a printed blog post. Attached to it was a color photo—full face, big round eyes, pouty lips, flawless mocha skin, braided hair. My eyes widened as I stared at the picture and wondered if my lack of sleep was affecting my mind.

My expression must have been an indication of my confusion, because Millie softly said, "Mr. Hill, is something wrong?"

I glanced at her, snatched the photo from the folder, and held it up. "Who is this?"

She frowned slightly. "Uh...Greer Kennedy, sir."

"Who?"

"Greer Kennedy. The travel blogger I'm meeting this morning."

I leaned back in my chair. "This is the Nubian Nomad?"

She nodded. "Yes."

I placed the photo on my desk and stared at it. So many things made sense to me at that moment—all of the pictures she took at the festival and the fact that she was there alone. Monique was really Greer, and she'd be in the Sable Inc. office, *my* office, in just a couple of hours.

"Why do you have her picture in here?"

"So I will recognize her when she arrives."

A smile inched across my face as I handed the folder back to her. "Everything looks great, Millie."

She smiled. "Thank you. I'm really excited about this proposed partnership."

"So am I. As a matter of fact, I believe I'll sit in on your meeting."

"Uh...sir?"

"This is still your baby, I just want to be there. I won't interfere."

She nodded. "Sure thing."

As she left, I said, "And Millie, please accept my apology for biting your head off earlier."

"Of course, sir."

I watched the door close behind her and then chuckled to myself. The day was shaping up to be much better than I ever could've imagined.

18

Greer

Back in the boardroom...

"Greer?"

"Now you know why I let you call me Monique."

"No, I like it. It suits you—unique, elegant..."

"I don't know about elegant. It's my mother's maiden name. Her name was Charlene Greer before she married my father. Mine is Greer Charlene."

"Hmm, I just learned more about you in the last five minutes than I did in those three days and four nights we spent together in my room."

I dropped my eyes from his face. "Look, I'm sorry to have wasted your time. I'll just...I'll just go and get out of your hair."

"Why would you want to do that? This was not a waste of my time. It's a good deal for both of us."

"I just thought—"

"Look, business is business, and what we did in Virginia? That was much more than business."

"Um...to be honest, I didn't hear a word that uh..."

"Millie."

"Yes, Millie. I didn't hear a word she said."

He smiled that smile of his and my insides began to melt again. "I've been a little distracted myself since I walked into this room and saw you, but I know the details of the deal well. I'd be more than happy to go over them with you over dinner so you can make a more informed decision."

"Derek—Mr. Hill, we can't move forward with this deal and you know it. Not with our...past."

"Our past?" he asked, his smile widening.

"Yes, you know. *Our past.*"

"You mean all the sex we had that I've been thinking about for the past two months, four days..." He paused to check his watch. "And five hours?"

I crossed my legs and tore my eyes away from his mouth. "Yes. How are we supposed to work together considering all of that?"

"Well, Ms. Kennedy, I'm the CEO, so you really won't be working with me that closely. You'll mostly work with Millie and her staff."

"Oh..."

"But that's not to say that we can't be...friends, or hopefully, much more than friends."

"I see..."

"So dinner? We can discuss business, and if you still feel the same, we can part ways. No hard feelings."

I closed my eyes and sighed. "Okay, dinner."

"Great, I'll send Millie back in and you can let her know where you're staying. I'll pick you up at five."

19

Greer

He picked me up in a limo.

A limo.

Came to my door in that damn suit looking like a good night's sex. He was smiling when I opened the door wearing a pant suit of my own, hoping the business attire would convey to him where my mind was. This dinner was about business and nothing else. I wasn't going to have it said that I got this deal on my back or my knees or his crotch…even if maybe I kind of sort of did. Or at least it seemed so since he knew who I was before I arrived at his office.

Or maybe not.

Hell, I was confused.

"You ready?" he asked as he stepped into the room, his cologne drifting in with him and making me dizzy.

I closed my eyes and inhaled deeply. That scent reminded me of Virginia, me and him, a memory I wanted to simultaneously dismiss and relish in at the same time. "Uh…yes. I am."

He reached for my hand. "Good."

I took his huge hand and let him lead the way. The ride to the restaurant, which he had declared was his favorite, was a quiet one, as I had no idea what to say. Sitting there next to him was assaulting my thought processes, leaving me with the intellect of a sweet potato. All I could think about was Virginia and Room 620 and his hands, his mouth, his—

"We're here," he said, interrupting my little trip down sexual memory lane.

"Oh…"

The restaurant was located on the top floor of a high rise building. We were seated near one of the floor-to-ceiling windows that provided a breathtaking view of downtown Houston. I was staring at the cityscape dotted with lights when he said, "Great view, isn't it?"

I shifted my eyes to him and nodded. "Yes, it's gorgeous."

"You should see the view from my office. It's even better."

"I bet it is. So you're a CEO. I wouldn't have guessed that."

"Why? Is it the dreads, or the earring, or the 'This is my shit,' or…other things."

"I don't know, maybe it was your hotel room. *My* room was better than yours, Mr. CEO. Are you a bit…frugal?"

He flashed me a smile. "Are you calling me cheap?"

I gave him a look of innocence. "No, no. Never that."

"It was a last-minute trip and our partner hotel in the area was booked solid. That room was the best I could get."

"Hmm, I see."

"You don't believe me?"

"Oh, I believe you. Unlike me, you disclosed your real name in Virginia. Takes an honest man to give his real name to a random sex partner."

"Is that how you see yourself?"

"Is it not the truth?"

"Not to me."

I felt warmth travel up my cheeks and took a quick sip of water.

"So I don't come off as a CEO, huh?"

I shrugged. "I don't know. I guess you just seem like the free and easy type of man rather than the corporate type."

"I see, well, I believe owning your own business is the absolute epitome of freedom."

"I would have to agree with that."

"Good. I'm glad we're starting this dinner out on common ground. So, what did you do before becoming the Nubian Nomad?"

"Don't you know? I mean, didn't you vet me before contacting me?"

He nodded. "Of course we did. Just humor me."

"Um…okay, I held a few clerical positions here and there. I also worked as a barista for a short while. Nothing major. I have a Psych degree from TSU I've never used. I even have a cosmetology license. I've kind of been all over the place, I guess. Never been afraid to try new things."

"Or travel to new places. A free spirit."

"Yes."

"But you found your success and a home of sorts with your blog."

"I did. Always loved to travel. My parents instilled that in me. So at first I would save money from whatever job I had and take little trips and share pictures on social media. Then I started blogging as a way of keeping a record of my adventures, and the next thing I knew, I had this huge following and people were contacting me about placing ads and offering me free trips. The rest is history."

"That's great, and I look forward to a future in partnership with you and your blog."

I took a breath and released it, then folded my hands in my lap, and said, "Look, um…I appreciate this, I really do, but I still can't accept your company's proposal."

"You would make that decision without hearing it? I know you said you were distracted during Millie's presentation."

"I was-I… fine. Let's hear it."

Over my corn risotto and his ribeye, he laid the terms out for me. Sable Jets would provide transportation for me to any destination—domestic or foreign—once monthly on one of their luxury jets. They would also arrange *and* pay for ground transportation and lodging at one of their partner establishments for up to three days. He threw out names like Hilton and Marriott but said there were many others. All Sable Jets wanted in return was for me to include pictures of the jet (inside and out) in the blog post for any trip that included a jet ride, as well as a banner ad and a linked, in-blog ad image. The banner ad was to remain on my blog for the duration of the partnership.

Under different circumstances, I would have been excited. Hell, I *was* excited but I was also despondent because there was no way I could work with him. As bad as I wanted this deal, and I really, really wanted it, that desire paled in comparison to my desire to screw this man, right then and right there on that table. I wanted to toss decorum out the door, rip my clothes off, climb up on that table on all fours, and throw my ass at him for as long as he could take it with all of those nicely-dressed, well-behaved patrons staring at us. As he spoke about a G-something-or-other jet, I wanted to lick his neck and plunge my tongue into his mouth. No, there was no way on earth we could work together on any level, even if it wasn't one-on-one, because he was too fine and I had prior knowledge of just how good he was in bed in the form of vivid images that played before me like a movie scene.

"So…what do you think? You still don't want to work with us?" he asked as he concluded his pitch.

"I think the proposal is-is excellent and it exceeds my expectations, but I cannot partner with you."

He frowned slightly, rested his folded hands on the table. "Can I ask why?"

I leaned forward and in a hushed voice said, "Mr. Hill, you know why."

"No…I don't, Ms. Kennedy."

I squeezed my eyes shut. "Yes, you do," I hissed.

He smiled. "Say it."

"Say what? I already said it's because of our past."

"The past where we screwed each other's brains out? The same past where I gripped your ass and licked your back?"

My mouth flew open.

"Oh, I guess that wasn't very business-like, was it? Let me rephrase, Ms. Kennedy. Are you referring to the innumerable intimate relations we shared in Virginia?"

"You know I am. And let me tell you this: I don't like this game you're playing."

"What game?"

"This game where you try to make me squirm."

"Am I making you squirm?"

I scooted back in my chair and sprung to my feet. "I'm not a damn kid. I'm a grown-ass woman, and you can go to hell with your little game. I'm not accepting your offer, and I hope to never see or speak to you again." I kept my voice low enough that those around us shouldn't have heard me, but my body language spoke volumes.

He stood and moved to my side of the table, placed his hand gently on my arm sending sparks to my core. I wished I hadn't taken my jacket off and hung it on my chair. His effect on me was unnerving, and I needed to be in control of myself. His touching me made that hard.

With his face so close to mine that I could feel heat radiating from it, he softly said, "I'm sorry. I truly am. It was not my intention to offend you in any way."

I inhaled his cologne and tried not to swoon. "Well, you did."

"I can see that, and I'm offering you my deepest apologies, Ms. Kennedy. I don't want to play games with you. That's the last thing I want to do. Will you please sit back down for a moment?"

I slowly shifted my eyes to his face, thought about how his lips felt on my…everything.

"*Please?*"

I pulled away from him and reclaimed my seat.

He sat down and straightened his already straight tie, glanced around the room. "I understand your misgivings. I really do. Will you at least allow me to show you one of our jets? I can have the driver take us to the airfield, right onto the tarmac. You won't have to get out of the car. I think if you see one, you might have a change of heart."

I fixed my eyes on the table and resisted the urge to rub the spot on my arm he had touched. "Mr. Hill…"

"Just a quick ride and then I'll take you back to your hotel and you can go back to your life and forget we ever met."

I sighed. "All right."

The jet—one of a fleet of six—was gorgeous and huge, and the thought of it ascending into the sky just for little old me was thrilling. So I sat in the limo on the tarmac of Sable Jets' small airfield located on the outskirts of Houston, and said, "I'd like to look at the contract again."

He grinned. "We can do that right now at my office. You're really going to love the view."

*****

"This truly is a great view," I said, standing before a wall of windows in Derek's office after having read over the contract.

"It's even more impressive when the office is dark. May I?"

"Sure."

He turned the bright overhead lights off, causing the lights from neighboring buildings and the street below to almost glow. I stared at the view for a moment before turning my attention back to his luxurious office space. "So this is where you do all your work?"

He nodded. He was standing by his desk with his hands in the pockets of his slacks, his eyes on me. "Yes, it is. Sometimes I sleep here. The couch is rather comfortable."

"You're a workaholic?" I asked as I moved toward the desk, fondled the nameplate sitting on it.

"I try to balance it out with my fair share of pleasure."

"Like Virginia?"

"Oh, that was much more than pleasure. Much, much more." He walked around the desk and stood next to me. "That was ecstasy."

I backed away from him a bit. "Really?"

"Yes, don't you agree?"

"Maybe..."

"I wish I could experience that again."

I lifted a brow. "Do you?"

"You have no idea how badly I do."

I turned my back to him and faced the window again. "How can we do that? I want this deal, but I don't want it to be about us. I want this because I earned it, not because of what we shared."

"One has nothing to do with the other. Millie found your blog and presented the idea to me. I okayed it before I realized who you were. Just give it a chance. One chance. I think it would be beneficial to both of us."

"It almost sounds like you're talking about me and you rather than our mutual business interests."

"I'm referring to both. I want to do business with you, Greer. But I have no intention of that being our only connection. I don't think we reconnected by accident. This was meant to happen. So...yes, I want you to give both me and Sable Jets a chance."

"I don't know…"

"What are you so afraid of, Greer?"

"You. I'm afraid of you, Mr. Hill."

He moved close enough to touch me, but didn't. "Don't be. Give me a chance. I promise I'll be good to you on both fronts, *very* good. Take a chance on me, Ms. Kennedy."

I stepped out of his reach and tilted my head to the side, appraising him in his suit. The familiar throbbing of my sex was clouding my mind a bit, but I knew what I wanted both in business and in pleasure, despite my fears. So I walked back over to his desk and said, "Okay."

He gave me a surprised look. "Okay for business or okay for us?"

I smiled slyly as I shrugged out of my jacket and unbuttoned my pants, letting them fall to the floor at my feet. I stepped out of them and responded with, "Okay for both."

I eased his jacket from his broad shoulders and helped him out of his shirt and tie. With his eyes following my every move, he reached down to unbuckle his belt, but I stopped him. "No, let me," I said.

He raised both of his hands in surrender, his eyes glued to mine.

I unbuckled his belt, unbuttoned his pants, and eased them down his muscular thighs before reaching into his briefs and wrapping my hand around his stiff shaft. He sucked in a breath as I slowly massaged him. Then his mouth met mine and he pulled my bottom lip between his and gently suckled it, took his hand and raked everything off of his desk before lifting me and placing me on it. Stepping between my open legs, he devoured my mouth with his while stroking my sex through the fabric of my panties.

"Ah!" I said into his mouth.

"Stand up," he murmured.

I did, and watched as he squatted before me and removed my panties, then he pulled my blouse over my head, and said, "You are so beautiful."

"And you are so damn fine," I said, breathily.

He reached around and unfastened my bra as if he'd been trained to do it before lifting me again and sitting me back on the desk, pulling me to the edge. He kneaded one breast while flicking the nipple of the other with his tongue. I closed my eyes and leaned back on my elbows and tried to catch my breath. When he entered me unexpectedly, I released a startled scream of pleasure.

"Ooooooh! Derek!"

"Call me Mr. Hill. I like that shit."

"Mr. Hill! Mr. Hill-Mr. Hill-Mr. Hill!"

He filled me completely, grinding to a rhythm only he could hear and only I could match.

"Baby!" he shouted. "Shit, I missed you!"

"I missed you, too." I sat up and found his mouth, kissed him deeply then grabbed his bottom lip and held it between my teeth, dug my nails into his back as he plunged deeper and deeper inside of me.

After several minutes, I pushed against his chest, and said, "Wait, sit down."

"What?" he asked between labored breaths.

"Sit down, Mr. Hill...on the couch. I wanna see just how comfortable it is."

With raised eyebrows, he said, "Oh," and took a seat on the couch.

I straddled him, used my hand to guide his erection inside of me, and eased down on it with a gasp as he gripped my ass and I gripped his shoulders. At first I was slow and steady with my grinding, but the longer I looked into his eyes and the more I felt his hands slide up and down my back, the more I quickened my pace until I eventually placed my feet on the couch on either side of him and began bouncing up and down on his rock-hard shaft with my head thrown back and deep hums of pleasure escaping my throat.

"Greer...Greer...baby..." he murmured as he suckled on my left breast.

"You like that, baby?" I asked with my eyes closed, on the edge of an internal explosion.

He pulled me close and matched my thrusts with his own. "Hell. Yeah."

20

Greer

Derek and I lay entwined in bed in my hotel room, both of us exhausted from round three of lovemaking that night. It was actually early the next morning, well before the sun was to rise and I was feeling, as Maxwell would say, fortunate. I can't lie. I was happy to be with him, and I wanted to keep being with him in any way I could. I was also happy at the prospect of partnering with his company. I just hoped things would work out on both ends.

My phone buzzed on the bedside table and I instinctively knew it was Trevia. I had talked to her earlier when I was getting ready for dinner and had been ignoring her calls for hours. I knew if I didn't answer, she was liable to send the police to my room to check on me. So I waited until "missed call" popped up on my screen and I texted her:

Me: *I'm fine. Will call u later.*
Trevia: *Ans ur phone. I'm calling back now.*

I rolled my eyes when her name appeared on the screen again, accepted the call, and whispered, "I'm fine. I'll call you later."

"What happened?!" she virtually screamed into the phone. She was evidently loud enough to wake Derek, because the next thing I knew, his eyes had popped open.

"Sorry," I whispered to him.

"Who you whispering to?" she asked, equally as loud.

"Look, I gotta go, Trevia."

Derek disappeared under the covers and a second later, I felt his tongue caressing my pearl.

"Oooooh, shit! Girl, I gotta goooooo," I groaned as I ended the call and dropped the phone on the floor. I gripped the back of his head and said, "If...you wanted...me to...hang up...you could've...just...asked..."

*****

"What made you want to get into the business of chartering jets?" I asked him the next morning over breakfast. I was sitting at the table in my room wearing my robe. He was naked, sitting on the side of the bed enjoying his food. As enticing as he looked, I was determined to concentrate on our conversation and get to know this man for more than his ability to set my body on fire.

He shrugged as he took a sip of his coffee. "I've always liked planes. It's kind of an obsession of mine. At one time I wanted to be an airline pilot, but I have this thing where I hate working for other people. So I decided to expand the company my father left to me and my brother to include Sable Jets. I saw a market that was untapped—rich black people who wanted the luxury of private air travel and were also committed to supporting black-owned businesses. Things took off pretty quickly."

"Can you fly a plane?"

"No, never got around to learning that. I wish I had, but owning several planes is a good consolation prize."

"You always travel via your jets?"

He nodded. "Always."

"So your father left you a business? What kind of business?"

"Well, the original Sable Inc. owned a chain of grocery stores here in the south. Ever heard of Olsen's?"

I frowned slightly. "Yeah, but I never knew they were black-owned."

"They weren't until my father bought the entire chain. Used the money he won from a settlement. He worked for the railroad for several years before suing them for discrimination after being unjustly passed over for promotion after promotion. After he bought the chain, he chose not to reveal ownership. After he died, Brandon and I decided to keep it as is but to expand the company to include other interests."

"Like what?"

"Sable Publishing owns *Sable Woman* and *Black King* magazines. And there's Black Stallion Contraceptives."

"You own a condom company?"

He smiled. "Yes, we do. It's the only brand I use."

I blushed. "Um, okay…why the names Sable Inc. and Sable Jets?"

"Sable was my mother's name."

"Oh, that's a beautiful tribute to her."

"Yes, she was a great woman and my father was a great man who adored her. They died ten years ago within months of each other."

"I'm so sorry…"

"It's okay. Now let's see…I'm six-four, my birthday is January fifth, I'm the youngest of two. My brother is six years older than me. I'm thirty-one, by the way. Never been married. No kids. Graduated from Prairie View with a degree in Business Administration. I was born and raised here in Houston. I like Neo Soul and R&B. I drink socially. I have excellent credit. I earn a great living, and I really, really like you."

I smiled. "Thanks for the résumé."

"I figured I'd lay it all out for you, because I've got to be at the office in a couple of hours, so that means I don't have long to get another taste of you before I head out to shower and change. I can't show up at my own company in yesterday's clothes, you know? Plus, you have another meeting with Millie this morning to seal the deal. So, why don't you come over here and sit on my lap?"

I tossed my napkin into my plate, stood, and shrugged out of my robe. "I'm more than happy to oblige you, but don't you want me to tell you about myself?"

"Of course I do. But later." He nodded toward his crotch. "We have other pressing matters to attend to right now."

*****

This man just had a way of making me change my plans.

After hashing everything out with Millie, I should've hopped a plane back home and started planning my itinerary for the rest of the year since I now had access to the private jet of my choice, but all it took was him asking me to stay, and I did. I would've stayed even if he hadn't offered to pay for my room. He wined me and dined me and sexed me every single night. My days were spent sleeping, because he usually kept me up all night. He was insatiable, but so was I when it came to what he had to offer. Just being in the room with him kept me in a constant state of moistness. I had never experienced anything as intense as the attraction we shared, and it made me question whatever feelings I thought I had for Lloyd. Whatever it was, it wasn't even in the same area code as what I felt for Derek. Was I falling in love or just totally blinded by lust? It was hard to differentiate. But one thing was for sure: I didn't want it to end. The more I learned about him, the more I liked about him. I could easily see myself spending the rest of my life with him.

I'd told him almost everything about me, from me being an only child to my obsession with traveling to my love for blogging. He listened intently, seemed genuinely interested, which was more than I could say about any other man I'd ever been involved with. On the final night of my stay in Houston, as I lay in his arms breathless from another round of lovemaking, I brushed my lips against his bare chest, and said, "I think I'm falling for you."

He kissed my forehead and rubbed my shoulder. "Hmm, I already fell for you, broke my leg, broke my hip, got a concussion…"

I laughed. "That bad?"

"No, that good. I can't get enough of you, Greer. I don't want to get enough of you."

"I feel the same way."

"And I know you've got to return to your life, but I don't want you to go. I don't want us to be apart."

"Me either, but you can come see me. After all, we live in the same state. It's a big-ass state, but we're only three hours away from each other, quicker for you since you own a whole fleet of jets."

He chuckled. "My jets are your jets, baby."

"You know what it does to me when you call me baby?"

"Probably the same thing it does to me when you call me Mr. Hill. Hey, can I ask you something?"

I closed my eyes. "Yeah, anything,"

"Where's your ring?"

My eyes popped back open. "What?"

"The ring you were wearing in Virginia. It looked like an engagement ring. What happened to it?"

"Uh…well, it *was* an engagement ring, but the engagement ended shortly before I got to Virginia. It just took me a while to take it off."

"So it's over now?"

"Very over. I gave it back to him." Well, that was sort of true.

"Good, and for the record, whoever he is, he's a damn fool, but his foolishness is my good fortune."

"Hmm, thanks for saying that."

He tightened his arm around me. "I meant every word. You're smart, beautiful, and excuse my language, but you have the best pussy I've ever had. So, yeah…he's a damn fool."

I lifted my head. "You must want to go for round four, because that just turned me the hell on."

"Baby, we can do it all night if that's what you want."

I climbed on top of him, and said, "There you go calling me baby again…"

21

Greer

I was still in bed, fast asleep, when the sound of my front door opening and closing awakened me. I sat up and strained my ears, reached for the knife I kept under my mattress and braced myself. A few seconds later, Denise appeared in my bedroom doorway.

"I'm really gonna have to take that damn key," I muttered as I scratched my head through my silk bonnet.

"Well then, I guess your ass should learn how to call people and let them know you made it home safely."

"I got home after midnight. It's only—" I glanced at the clock at my bedside. "Shit, it's after eleven?"

"Yes, heifer, and if Trevia wasn't tracking Wesley like a damn bloodhound, she'd be here, too."

I rubbed my forehead. "Lord, what's going on with them now?"

"Who the hell knows? Now tell me what happened in Houston."

"Trevia didn't tell you already?" I asked through a yawn.

"She told me that Virginia sex dude owns the jet company and she was pretty sure she caught you screwing him."

"I just can't have any privacy in my life, can I?"

She leaned against the door facing with an expectant look on her face.

"Derek is the CEO of Sable Inc. and..."

She folded her arms over her chest and leaned forward. "And what?"

"And I signed the contract. I'm partnering with Sable Jets, and girl, the deal is the bomb!"

"Girl, I don't give a damn about that! What happened with *him*?"

I rolled my eyes. "We...uh, we have an understanding."

"Okay..."

"Oh, hell. You know I stayed longer than expected."

"Yeah?"

"Well, I spent that time doing the nasty with Mr. Derek Hill!"

She rushed over to my bed and sat at the foot. "I knew it! So y'all are a thing now?"

"Yes, we are."

"Still no pictures of him?"

I grabbed my phone from beside me on the bed and scrolled to a picture I took of him on the Tarmac before I boarded his jet to return home.

Denise stared at the phone. "Daaaaamnnnn. I hope you got his number this time, because fine like this is hard to come by."

"I got his number, email, you name it."

"I know that's right. I'm so happy for you. Lloyd ain't got shit on Mr. CEO."

I smiled and then started laughing.

"What's so funny?"

"I can't tell you the last time I thought about Lloyd. It's like I totally forgot that we were together and engaged two months ago."

"That's when you know the penis is stellar. The man done gave you amnesia."

I fell back onto the bed and laughed, but she was right. Derek Hill and all of his goodness had all but erased Lloyd from my memory.

*****

"Trevia, when you get this, give me a call, okay? I'm worried about you."

I'd been home a week and was finalizing plans to travel to a literary festival, but I couldn't shake this bad feeling I was having about Trevia. I hadn't seen or heard from her since I'd been back and that definitely wasn't like her. What alarmed me more was that neither her sister nor Denise had heard from her either. I'd even tried to reach Wesley to no avail. I really hoped nothing had happened to her.

I sighed and decided to check my email before figuring out what I was going to eat for lunch. I scrolled through the new, unread messages—spam, newsletters I'd subscribed to, and one from Adventure Airlines. I frowned as I opened it and scanned the message.

Greer,

I hope you're doing well. I need to meet with you as soon as possible. In person. Please reply with a day and time that's good for you.

Thanks,

Lloyd

I spent the next hour obsessing over the email, wondering if it sounded as personal as I thought it did or if I was imagining that, or maybe I just wanted it to sound personal because I still loved him. That couldn't be it, could it? I had Derek. Derek with the good body, great face, and exquisite penis.

No, I definitely wasn't in love with Lloyd. Not at all.

"Okay, I'll bite," I said to myself.

Lloyd,

You can meet me at Dardenne's tomorrow at 5PM.

Greer

22

Derek

I was at my desk, staring out the window instead of tackling the work in front of me. I'd been doing that a lot in the week since Greer left. If it was up to me, she wouldn't have left at all. It felt crazy to think that, but it was exactly what I desired—to be with her all day, every day.

I had never met anyone like her. Adventurous, smart, independent, sexy, everything I ever wanted in a woman. I'd never felt so connected to a woman before, never wanted anyone or anything as badly as I wanted her at that moment. Was I in love with Greer Kennedy? That was the only logical explanation for what I was feeling, but how could I share my feelings with her without scaring her away? It had taken using my best negotiation skills to convince her to even give me a chance. She'd just been hurt. If I moved too fast, I was sure I'd ruin things.

I would have to move slowly—court her, make sure she felt my love before I declared it to her verbally.

"Knock, knock."

I shifted my attention from the window to the door where my brother stood with some papers in his hand.

"What's up, Mr. Hill?" I asked.

He crossed the room and sat in front of my desk. "We need to go over this marketing deal you okayed with Millie."

I sighed. Brandon was the CFO by choice, and he was an obsessive micromanager of the company's finances. I was an unapologetic risk-taker while Brandon was cautious to a fault. I suppose I had him to thank for the company's financial stability and success. But his second-guessing my decisions despite my proven track record was irritating as hell.

"It's a sound investment, Brandon. Did you read the blog stats? 50,000 unique visitors per week. Hundreds of thousands of subscribers. Nearly one million in social media reach. She's written travel articles for *Ebony* and *Essence*. It's good exposure for us."

"But is it the right demographic? Can this woman's followers afford to charter our jets?"

"What Millie and I discussed is that we'll gear the ads toward group charters. You know, a group of friends sharing the cost of a trip. Plus, the blog has a small celebrity following according to Millie. Greer receives invitations to some exclusive events, and she will stand out arriving via our sponsored ground transportation. And don't forget about the publications she's written for. There's a good chance she could be invited to write for them again while partnering with us."

Brandon shook his head. "I don't believe this. It's true."

I straightened in my chair and with a furrowed brow, said, "What?"

"You have a thing for the blogger. I heard you couldn't take your eyes off of her during the meeting."

"Heard from who?" I was shocked. I'd never seen Millie as a gossiper.

"The office rumor mill. And then you took her to dinner? God only knows what else you did with her while she was here."

"What's your point?"

"Your judgment is clouded. Who is this woman? What was it, love at first sight or something in the boardroom?"

I sighed as I tugged at my tie. "I've met her before."

The room fell silent. A minute or two later, Brandon said, "Virginia."

I nodded.

"Shit, no wonder."

"Look, I didn't know it was her when I okayed the deal."

"Damn, Derek. You can't do this."

"It's only a six-month deal. Six months. Six trips that we'll be covering. If we see where it's not benefitting the company, we don't have to continue. When have you ever known me to hold on to something that wasn't working?"

Brandon rubbed his forehead. "Okay, I hear you, but Derek, we're absorbing the costs of fuel, paying the pilot, ground transportation, hotel...We're going to be hemorrhaging money for six months!"

"Did you look at the cost comparison of this deal as opposed to running TV and magazine ads in publications other than our own?"

"Yes, but—"

I slapped my hand on the desk. "Look, Brandon! The deal stands even if I have to pay for it out of my own pocket!"

Brandon stared at me. "Shit, you're in love with this woman."

I didn't reply. Hell, I *couldn't* reply.

"You're going to *have* to do something about Sasha now if you want a future with this woman. And from what I can see, you definitely want a future with her."

"I know. I'm still trying to figure that one out."

"Well, you better figure it out quickly. A secret baby's mama will definitely ruin things."

"I don't know that she's my baby's mama, B."

"Then why is she living in your house while you sleep here and there and everywhere?"

"Because I'm not a bad person. Her house burned and she lost her job. My baby or not, I wasn't going to let her be homeless."

"How'd she manage to run into that much bad luck at the same time? She's scamming you, bro."

"She probably is, but I'm going to fix it."

"You better." He held the papers up and added, "And you better be right about this deal."

"When am I ever wrong when it comes to Sable Inc.?"

"You do have a point." He stood to leave. "Hey, I'm glad you found someone who makes you happy."

"She does, Brandon. She really does."

"Good. You deserve it."

*****

I unlocked my front door, entered my house, and for the first time since Sasha moved in, I actually hoped she was home. Instead of me dealing with things as I had in the past, which amounted to not dealing with them at all, I was going to handle this situation with her. Brandon was right. I had to know the truth about Sasha's baby before things went any further with Greer. If she found out about this crazy arrangement, I'd lose her before she was truly mine.

I found her in the living room, curled up on the couch sleeping with the TV on the Lifetime Channel. There was an empty plate and glass on the coffee table. Something about seeing her so relaxed in my home, when I knew I couldn't bring Greer there because of her pissed me off, so I shouted, "Sasha!"

She sprung up and instantly placed her hand protectively on her stomach. "What's going on?" she asked, her eyes darting around the room.

"What's your price?" I asked.

She looked even more confused. "What?"

I moved to the loveseat situated adjacent to the couch and sat down. "Look, you love money, especially *my* money. I've always known that, because you've made it perfectly clear. That's why you've decided this baby is mine and not that random guy you cheated with. You want the baby to be mine because of my money."

"Derek—"

"I want the test done, Sasha. I need to know for sure if that's my baby. If it's not, I'll help you get a place. Hell, I'll help you find a job, too, but if that is not my child, I want you out of my life. For good."

A single tear trickled down her cheek. "I can't believe this. I'm not lying. This is your baby."

"Prove it. Let's do the paternity test. ASAP."

"I don't want to. I want you to trust me."

"I can't. Now, name your price. How much do I need to pay you in order for you to agree to take this test?"

She rubbed her belly again. "What kind of person are you? You never ask about me or the baby. You just storm in and out of here like I'm some inconvenience."

"Name. Your. Price."

She narrowed her eyes. "Fine. Fifty thousand."

"Okay, I'll let you know when I get the appointment scheduled."

"You are going to regret treating me like this."

As I left without responding to her threat, I heard her scream, "I hate you!"

23

Greer

I was filled with apprehension when I entered the restaurant and spotted Lloyd sitting at a table near the back. I was so anxious, I wordlessly side-stepped the greeter and headed straight for the table. He looked the same—tall, neat, well-dressed, handsome, but sitting at that table with him felt so...odd. It almost felt like we hadn't seen each other in years rather than a few months. Whatever I thought I felt for him at one time was a distant memory, because I can honestly say I felt nothing for him as I sat there but regret for having wasted my time with him. The only thought in my mind was there were a ton of more productive things I could've been doing at that moment. Why had I agreed to this meeting?

"Thank you for agreeing to meet me."

I stared at him.

"And I'm sorry about the deal with your blog. I just couldn't get the powers that be to jump on board with it."

"What do you want? Because I know we're not here about my blog."

He locked his eyes on me. "Straight to the point, huh? Same old Greer. You don't want a drink or anything?"

"Why are we here, Lloyd?"

"Okay, first, I want to apologize to you again now that we're face to face. I'm sorry for the way I handled things."

"Things?"

"With us. I'm sorry about the way I handled things with us."

"I think the point is you *didn't* handle things. At all."

He nodded as he dropped his eyes to his hands, which rested on the table. "You're right. I was...I was afraid to tell you, but I was going to tell you. It just so happened that you found out before I could."

"Lloyd, you ignored my calls after blocking me on Facebook. You had obviously already moved on without bothering to tell me anything. Your actions were the reason I found out. Your actions also showed me you had no intentions of ever telling me a damn thing. If you are going to sit here and lie to me, I'm leaving because believe me, I have much better shit I could be doing right now."

"Okay...I'm sorry. Look, I was a coward. I messed up."

"That's all you have to say? That's why you wanted to see me? Lloyd, we could've done this over the phone."

"But then I wouldn't be able to see your beautiful face."

I grabbed my purse. "Screw this."

"Wait! I need to know if you forgive me. I-I need you to forgive me...for everything."

I frowned and leaned back in my seat. "What?"

"I'm supposed to get married soon, but I don't think I can do it with this unfinished business hanging over my head, Greer. I need to hear you say you forgive me."

I tilted my head to the side and scoffed. "You're having second thoughts."

"I didn't say that—"

"But that's it. You messed up and now you're feeling it. Well, you shouldn't have gotten her pregnant while you were still with me!" The couple at the table next to ours was gawking at me, but I didn't care.

"Can you keep your voice down?" he asked, embarrassment and shock shrouding his face.

"Couldn't you keep your thing in your pants?"

"Okay, I deserved that."

"You deserve worse."

"How do you know about the baby?"

"Don't worry about how I know."

"Greer, I—"

"You know what? I don't forgive your sleazy ass. You were sleeping with us both and you got her pregnant, which means you weren't using any protection with *Tami*. If I had fallen for that we're-engaged-and-you're-on-birth-control-so-we-don't-need-to-use-condoms crap you tried to pull, there's no telling what disease you might have given me. Or worse, my ass could be pregnant and chained to you for the next eighteen years! The hell is wrong with you?"

"Maybe we shouldn't have met in such a public place..."

"Maybe you shouldn't be such an ass."

"Greer, I still love you."

"Oh, what a coincidence. I still love my damn self. As a matter of fact, I love myself enough to leave right now and never look back." I shot to my feet, purse in hand. "Go to hell, Lloyd Ray Robinson, and never, *ever* contact me again."

"Greer—"

I made my exit without giving him a backwards glance.

*****

"How was the literary festival?" Derek asked as I held the phone with one hand and dug through my refrigerator with the other. I was hungry but needed to buy groceries. I'd been ordering take-out for weeks, and I was quite frankly tired of spending so much money. I actually enjoyed cooking but despised the grocery store.

I sighed, glanced at the dozen roses in my trash can—a gift Lloyd had delivered to my apartment, the only contact he'd made in the two weeks since our little meeting—and left the kitchen when I realized my search for food was fruitless. As I plopped down on my bed and stared at the ceiling, I said, "It was great. Those readers know how to party."

"Good. I'm glad you had a good time. I trust your flights were comfortable?"

"Yes, Mr. Hill. The flights, the limo, and the hotel were all great. I can't wait for you to read my blog. I'm even including a video tour of the jet."

"Really? I'd love to see that."

"Yeah, I think I'm going to start doing some vlogs. They're pretty popular now."

"Sounds like a great idea. So, what did you have for dinner?"

"Nothing yet? You?"

"Nothing for me either. I'm working late, probably have something delivered. What do you have a taste for?"

"Why? You gonna come cook for me?"

"I wish I could. I make a mean boiled hot dog."

I chuckled. "Hmm, well, I don't have a taste for a hot dog, but I'd love to have a huge burger from The Kitchen Sink."

"The Kitchen Sink?"

"Yeah, their slogan is, 'We put everything in our burgers including the kitchen sink.'"

He laughed. "I see. What's your favorite thing to eat there?"

"The meatloaf burger is too good for words. Damn, I wish they delivered. I don't feel like going out to get it."

"If I was there, I'd bring you one."

"If you brought me one, I'd definitely show you my appreciation."

"Really? How?"

"Hmm, I'd strip you..."

"Yeah..."

"And kiss you..."

"Would you?"

"Mm-hmm. And lick you..."

"Where?"

"Wherever you want me to."

"Shit!"

"What?"

"I've got another call, baby. I've got to go. Hey, I'm gonna come see you next week if that's okay with you."

"It's more than okay."

After we ended the call, I lay in bed thinking of Derek, my body on fire. In teasing him, I'd messed myself up, but I was too tired and famished to do anything about it.

Two hours later, I was still in the exact same spot on my bed, having fallen asleep. When my eyes popped open, I wasn't sure what awakened me. It took me a full two minutes to recognize the sound that had ripped me from my sleep as knocking at my door. I climbed out of bed and shuffled to the door, knowing it was either Denise or Trevia, since they were the only people who ever visited me. Maybe they'd finally decided to respect me enough not to just use their keys and barge in on me. Still, it could've been another delivery from Lloyd, but if that was the case, I was going to be pissed the hell off at having my sleep disturbed for that crap.

"Who is it?!" I yelled through the door, unable to see anyone through the peephole.

"Delivery for Ms. Kennedy."

I rolled my eyes, deciding I was going to call and curse Lloyd out as soon as possible. I snatched the door open and clamped my hand over my mouth at the sight of a gorgeous man in a three-piece suit standing before me holding a huge plastic sack from The Kitchen Sink. "Derek? I thought you were in Houston."

He closed the space between us and softly kissed my lips. "I was. Decided to bring you dinner. Now what was that about kissing and licking?"

I smiled as I led him into my home.

Once inside, I put the food in the kitchen and joined him in the living room where he was perusing the photos of me, my friends, and my parents on the end table. I stepped behind him and wrapped my arms around his waist. "I'm so glad you're here," I whispered.

He placed his hands on my arms and leaned against me. "So am I. I missed you." He turned to face me. "Ready to eat?"

I shook my head. "I need to repay you first."

He grinned. "Okay..."

I kissed him lightly on the lips and then fell to my knees before him, freeing him of his pants and underwear. His erect penis bounced in front of my face. I held it in my hand, wrapped my lips around the head, and gently suckled. I felt Derek's hand on the back of my head, heard him whisper, "Baby..."

I lavished the length of him with my tongue before taking him into my hot mouth. Massaging his shaft with my hand, I slid him in and out of my mouth while swirling my tongue around and around him. His agonizing moans filled the room as he swayed a bit, steadily growing louder, coarser. A few minutes later, he moved backwards, causing his shaft to slip from my mouth. He reached for my hand and helped me to my feet, kissed me, and murmured, "My turn," then led me to the couch where he kneeled before me and spread my legs. I closed my eyes as he slid his tongue over my bud. As he tortured me with his tongue while slipping a finger into my wetness, I gripped his head and fought not to scream.

When I thought I could take no more, he stopped, stood over me, and said, "Come here, baby."

I got to my feet on weak-as-hell legs, almost too spent to go any further, but he was not done with me. As he lifted me from the floor, I wrapped my legs around him and sucked in a breath when he penetrated me and began to thrust deeper and deeper.

I clawed at his back, screamed, "Derek!"

"Ah! Greer!"

I closed my eyes as the pressure inside of me built to the point of no return. When I felt my walls begin to quiver, I screamed, "Baby!"

"I know," he grunted. "Me too, baby…"

*****

Two hours slid by before we got around to eating the burgers Derek brought. The good thing about The Kitchen Sink's burgers is they tasted just as good reheated as they did fresh off the griddle. We sat on the floor, half-clothed and exhausted from getting reacquainted. Or at least *I* was exhausted. I wasn't sure if I'd ever seen Derek tired or not raring to go when it came to sex. I deduced he was one man who had taken very good care of his body.

"How did you get my address? From Millie?" I asked, as I tossed my empty burger wrapper onto the coffee table and lay on my side appraising this man who seemed to have memorized my body and innately knew my deepest desires.

"No, you gave it to me."

I frowned slightly. "Really? I don't remember giving it to you. When did this happen?"

"In your hotel room in Houston, the night after that first meeting. I seem to recall your legs being on my shoulders, and I think your exact words were: 'My name is Greer Charlene Kennedy, I was born on August seventh, I live at 1808 Arturo Boulevard in apartment 38C in Dallas, Texas, and I swear before God this pussy is yours!'"

I dropped my eyes for a brief moment. "I did say that, didn't I?"

He nodded and after taking a sip of soda, said, "Yeah, and since I've never had that happen before, it was hard to forget."

"So embarrassing..."

"No need to be embarrassed, but I do want to know if you meant it. Is it mine, Greer?"

"Mr. Hill, you've put your stamp, your brand, and your seal on it. It's definitely yours."

"I don't know if I believe that."

"Why not?"

"It's not like you told me your favorite color, favorite song, favorite movie, food, shoe size, credit score..."

I smirked. "Really?"

"Just saying."

"Okay, yellow, *A Long Walk* by Jill Scott, *Love Jones*, corn dogs with copious amounts of mustard, eight and a half, and you're gonna have to work for the credit score."

"Work for it, huh?"

"Yep. Now are you convinced that it's yours?"

"Yeah, I think I am, and you oughta know for damn sure you own every part of me."

"Really?"

"Really, baby."

"All right, well, quid pro quo, Mr. Hill—color, song, movie, food, shoe size, credit score."

He chuckled. "Okay, I guess that's fair. Color: black. Song: *Fortunate*, of course."

I nodded. "Of course. After all, that's your shit."

"Yes, that is indeed my shit. Movie: *Blue Hill Avenue*, food: steak, shoe—"

"That's enough. I'm convinced. No need in giving me the shoe size, because I know you wear some big ass shoes to go along with that big ol' thing between your legs."

He threw his head back and laughed. "Well, thank you, baby."

I smiled and scooted closer to where he was seated with his back against my sofa and rested my head on his lap. "Mm, I love that you're here."

"Me, too."

"So...you've seen my home in all its loud, IKEA-furnished glory. When do I get to see yours, Mr. Hill?"

After a moment of silence, he softly said, "Soon, baby. Soon."

24

Derek

It felt strange sitting in the waiting area of the doctor's office with Sasha. To everyone around us, we must've looked like an expectant couple, albeit an unhappy one. I could feel my brow in a constant furrow, and I could see Sasha out of the corner of my eye wringing her hands in her lap. She was nervous, probably afraid the baby wasn't mine, afraid the money train would end before it really began. If I didn't learn anything else from Sasha Porter in the six months we dated, I learned that she loved money, expensive gifts, and being on the arm of someone who could give those things to her.

We met at a Christmas party at my office. She was working as a temp at the time, but for some reason I never saw her around the office until that party. She was gorgeous in a red, figure-hugging dress with her honey-colored hair swept to one side contrasting flawless, deep mahogany skin. She had a bubbly personality and an infectious smile. For a while we were good. But while I consider myself a generous man, I couldn't deal with the little hints she started dropping about pieces of jewelry or purses she wanted, or her constantly complaining about her bills. I began feeling like a walking dollar sign when I was around her. And then she cheated on me. Crazy thing is, I actually caught her in the act so to speak. I went over to her place to surprise her with an early dinner date and there the guy was, leaving just as I pulled up to her house, kissing her right in the doorway. I was pissed, mostly because I'd never cheated on her. I'd always been a one-woman man like my pops. So, I dumped her, didn't hear from her again until she showed up at my doorstep homeless and pregnant two months later. I took her in, because I'm a good person, not because I loved her or ever had.

Greer was a different story.

We hadn't known each other that long, but I knew what I felt for Greer was well beyond the scope of like. It was honestly a feeling I'd never felt before, a feeling I couldn't adequately describe even if I was forced to at gunpoint. I just knew it felt good, better than anything I'd ever experienced, and I couldn't get enough or too much of it.

"Ms. Porter?" a nurse called.

Sasha dragged her eyes from her hands to my face. "I don't want to do this, and I don't have to."

"No, you don't *have* to, but I *need* you to. I need to know. I deserve to know either way, so I can go on with my life."

"You sure are in a hurry to be rid of me."

I patted the chest pocket of my suit. "If you want this check, you need to get up and go take that test."

She sighed and stood from her seat. "I hope whoever has you acting like this with me knows what a cold, unloving person you are and how you're trying to avoid taking responsibility for your child," she hissed.

I shook my head as I watched her follow the nurse through a door that quickly closed behind them. Twenty minutes later, I heard my name being called. It was my turn to provide a sample for the test.

25

Greer

After taking two trips as a Sable Jets partner, I was getting spoiled, but I suppose private jet rides, limo service, and luxury hotel rooms will do that. This deal beat using frequent flyer miles any day. I was truly enjoying the lushness of both my business life and my personal life. Nearly five months had passed since we first met in Virginia, and Derek and I were spending as much time as possible together with him traveling to Dallas nearly every weekend I was home. I loved being with him, exploring parts of my town with him, sharing my bed with him. Sure, he was a gorgeous man, but what I loved most about him was his heart and the way he treated me, the attention he showered me with. He was a man in every sense of the word, but he was also kind and gentle and so loving.

Loving.

Love.

Derek was becoming synonymous with those words, but I'd be lying if I said the heaviness of what I felt for him didn't frighten me. It petrified me because of the potential pain that would result from a break up. I'd been bruised by Lloyd's betrayal, and what I felt for him was nowhere as intense as what I was feeling for Derek. Lloyd was kind to me, but he was also somewhat detached. There was no real passion between us but rather a comfortable togetherness. We weren't all that compatible but agreed to disagree on lots of things. I had mistakenly seen Lloyd as a safe bet—steady, grounded, loyal. But Derek? He was much more than that to me. Derek was desire incarnate. Derek and I burned hot, scorching hot, and I thirsted for him. Without him, there would be a void inside of me that I wasn't sure anyone else could fill. How in the world would I ever recover if we didn't work out?

Speaking of Lloyd, I'd heard no more from him after our meeting and the lone delivery of flowers, thank goodness. According to Trevia, who had finally crawled out of hiding but refused to explain her disappearance, he and Tami were now married. All I could do was shrug. I honestly didn't care. How could I when I had Derek?

Derek.

I missed him although it had only been a few days since we were together. As I turned and gazed out the window of the sleek jet on my way to an event in New York, I fully realized and finally admitted to myself that I was totally and completely in love with Derek Dwight Hill, and I loved the way it felt.

I arrived at the venue a few minutes early to find the red carpet empty and wondered if I'd gotten the time wrong. Was I that early? The invitation I'd received via email was to a private premiere screening of the newest Will Smith movie. It didn't fit with my festival theme, but I wasn't a damn fool. I wasn't turning down an opportunity like this.

I was dressed in a tiny black cocktail dress and silver stilettos, and had hired a local make-up artist to beat my face into submission. I fully expected to be met by a crowd of screaming fans, flashing cameras, bustling reporters, and throngs of celebrities. But...nothing. Only an empty red carpet. I stared out the window in utter confusion, wondered if this was some practical joke. Was someone going to jump out of a dark corner with a camera and eventually plaster startled images of the Nubian Nomad being made a fool of all over the Internet? I wasn't sure what to do.

When the driver opened the door for me, I stepped out and asked, "Are you sure this is the right place?"

He nodded. "Yes, positive. This is the Gerwich Theater."

I sighed and checked the time on my cell phone. Perhaps I'd misunderstood when I was supposed to arrive, misread the invitation and arrived late rather than early. I decided to go inside, head straight to the ladies' room, and try to figure out what to do. Maybe I could slide into the back of the theater if need be. I had to try to make this work. After all, I didn't travel to New York to stay in my hotel room.

I walked the empty red carpet and one of the huge, ornate theater doors swung open. At first I thought it opened on its own, then I noticed the gentleman dressed as an old-time theater usher complete with a pillbox hat holding the door. He gave me a smile and a little bow. "Welcome."

"Hi, thanks," I said. "Um, has the movie already started?"

"No, Ms. Kennedy. They've been waiting for you to arrive."

"What?" How'd he know my name?

Before he could answer me, another usher appeared and offered me his arm. "Right this way, Ms. Kennedy."

I took his arm, too bewildered to do or say anything else.

He led me into the huge theater. The house lights were on, and I could see two people seated near the front. And there, standing on the stage before the wide, empty screen wearing a black tuxedo and holding a single red rose, was Derek.

Derek

My plan worked out perfectly, and to say she was surprised would be an understatement. I wasn't sure if she was more excited to see me or to meet Will and Jada. It paid to have connections in high places. We had featured Jada in *Sable Woman* magazine a few months earlier, and I was fortunate enough to be present for the photo shoot. We'd kept in touch, and when I contacted her with my plan, she had quickly jumped on board and brought her husband along with her. The four of us watched the movie together, and afterwards, Greer and I took a limo to a restaurant in Manhattan for a late dinner. After that, we headed to her hotel room.

Something had changed between us, or maybe a better way of putting it is there was a shift in our relationship. Our lovemaking that night was much more urgent and there was a deepened intensity to every touch, every sensation we shared. There was an ache inside of me that only left when I was with her, me in her arms and her in mine. At that moment, in that hotel room, I fully realized that Greer had transitioned from a want to a need. A great need. So when I reached the top of the mountain while holding her tightly to my body, I roared the words, "I love you!"

And it was a relief to hear her echo my words while clutching me and kissing my neck: "I love you, too…"

26

Greer

I was naked, bending over trying to make food appear in Derek's refrigerator when I heard, "Now that's the best sight I've ever seen in this kitchen."

I closed the door and placed my hands on my hips. "It took you forever to let me see this place, which means you had ample time to stock the kitchen, and lo and behold, you need groceries."

"There'll be food at the party."

"I know, but I wanted a snack. You're gonna have to do better with the food if I'm going to be spending time here."

"Glad you feel at home enough to make demands." Wearing a towel and a smile, he approached me, wrapped his arms around me, and pulled me to his wet chest.

I kissed it and gazed up at him.

"And how much time are you planning to spend here anyway?" he asked.

"As much as you want me to."

"I want you to move in."

I backed out of his arms. "Are you serious?"

"Very."

"Wow, um..."

"You don't have to decide right now. I know you have friends in Dallas and you've lived there all your life, but I love you, Greer, and I'm not myself unless I'm with you. I want you with me. Just think about it."

I leaned against the granite-top island and said, "I love you, too. I'll think about it."

The Sable Inc. annual Christmas party was held in the ballroom at Houston's historic Newmont Hotel. It was a black-tie affair, and I was so happy to be there with Derek, I nearly floated into the room in my flowing, beaded burgundy gown. Derek wore a black tuxedo with a white shirt and burgundy bow tie. We looked so good together, a matching set of melanated perfection, and I couldn't have been prouder to be on his arm. I had voiced my misgivings about being his date at first, because our business partnership was common knowledge amongst the employees. His response was, "Baby, I run the company. No one is going to check me, and they sure as hell better not even try to check you if they want to keep their job."

Well, that put my mind at ease. If he wasn't concerned, I wouldn't be either. I was going to eat, drink, dance, and be merry with the man I loved more than I knew I could love anyone.

We'd barely made it into the ballroom when we were approached by a couple I recognized as his brother and sister-in-law. He wore a white tuxedo. His wife wore a gorgeous red gown with a full skirt.

His brother, who on closer inspection greatly resembled Derek, smiled widely as he greeted me with, "I finally get to meet the famed Nubian Nomad. I'm Brandon Hill, and this is my beautiful wife, Vanessa."

I shook hands with both of them. "It's great to finally meet you."

"Same here," Brandon said. "And I want to personally congratulate you on the success of the Sable Jets partnership. We've booked nearly a dozen charter trips that listed the referral source as your blog."

"Wow, really?!" I gushed. This was definitely exciting news. I nudged Derek. "Why didn't you tell me?"

"I thought I did. Can't seem to think around you, baby."

I rolled my eyes and Brandon and Vanessa both laughed. "Well, we're going to make the rounds. Enjoy your night, Greer. And thanks for keeping this knucklehead in line."

They left and I asked, "Do you need to be kept in line, Mr. Hill?"

He shook his head, leaned in, and whispered, "Not since I met you. You whipped me into shape real quick with that piece of Heaven between your legs. As a matter of fact, I want to find a bathroom, take you in there, lift up this dress, and bend you over a sink right now."

Sister girl down there started throbbing again, but my growling stomach took precedence. "Feed me and I might just make that wish come true."

He smiled as he led me to the buffet tables set up on the far side of the room.

We made plates and sat at Derek's reserved table, which was

situated on the edge of the huge dancefloor and provided a good view of the stage where a band was playing old school R&B. The food was good, and the atmosphere was light. Several employees stopped by the table to greet Derek, who must've been tired of introducing me but never failed to do so. Once we were full and satisfied, we hit the dancefloor and tore it up! I'd never seen Derek move to an up-tempo song the way he did that night. The man was smooth, and I did my best to match his performance with one of my own. I knew I could dance, and judging from the approving look he gave me, Derek was impressed with my skills.

We took a break after about six songs and headed to our table. Derek left me long enough to get us some drinks, and shortly after he returned, handed me my drink and planted a long, lingering kiss on my lips. A voice interrupted our moment.

"Excuse me. I don't mean to disturb you, but I've been trying to find your table since I arrived."

My body stiffened from head to toe, and I snatched myself away from Derek and looked up at the body that held that voice.

Lloyd.

What the entire hell is he doing here?!

Derek gave me a confused look before turning his attention to Lloyd, who was gawking at me open-mouthed. "Oh, you made it? Great," Derek said.

He knew Lloyd? How? Why? What was going on?

"Greer, this is Lloyd Robinson, our new head of marketing. He comes to us from Adventure Airlines. Lloyd, this is the love of my life,

Greer Kennedy."

My stomach dropped and threatened to eject every morsel of food I'd eaten. "Uh..." was all I managed to say.

"Wow, love of your life? Those are strong words." Lloyd proffered his hand to me.

I took it for exactly a nanosecond before pulling away from him. "Um, excuse me," I mumbled. "I need to go to the ladies' room."

As I grabbed my clutch and stood to leave, Derek stood and gently grasped my arm, whispered, "You okay, baby?"

I nodded. "Yeah, I think I might've eaten too much. Be right back."

He cupped the sides of my face with his hands and kissed my lips. "Hurry back."

"I will."

I left, glancing back in time to see Lloyd take a seat at our table.

27

Greer

I ducked into the ladies' room and sat on a padded bench near the door. Derek had no idea who Lloyd was. I was sure of that, because I had never mentioned his name. I'd never even told him the circumstances of our break-up and he'd never asked. If I told him now he might feel obligated to fire him, which would easily set him up for a lawsuit as he really wouldn't have any grounds to fire him other than "he screwed over my woman." If I didn't tell him, I could look forward to a future of working with Lloyd since he was over marketing. That thought made me feel like vomiting again. I wasn't angry at Lloyd, nor did I hate him, but I damn sure wasn't trying to work that closely with him.

What was I supposed to do?

Maybe he'd quit. Surely he'd quit. He couldn't be looking forward to working with me any more than I was to working with him. Yes, he would quit. Maybe he already had!

I checked myself in a mirror before leaving the restroom and returning to the table to find that not only was Lloyd still there, but he'd been joined by Tami.

Well, shit.

I reclaimed my seat and leaned into Derek when he wrapped an arm around my shoulder. He kissed my cheek and asked, "You all right?"

I nodded as I crossed my legs and placed a hand on his knee. "I'm fine."

"Missed you."

"Missed you, too."

"Oh, baby, this is Lloyd's wife, Tami. Tami, this is my gorgeous, breathtaking lady and a Sable Inc. business partner, Greer Kennedy."

Wearing a strained expression on her puffy face, she offered me a weak *hi*.

"Hi," I said. "Wow, how far along are you?"

She looked uncomfortable as she replied. "I'm due in six weeks."

I shifted my eyes from her to Lloyd. "Congratulations."

They mumbled, "Thanks," almost in unison.

"You ready to hit the dancefloor again?" Derek asked.

"More than ready," I declared, as I hopped to my feet. Upon my urging, we stayed out on that dancefloor so long my feet were pulsating by the time we made it back to Derek's house, but I didn't care if they fell off as long as I didn't have to sit at that table with the Robinsons.

*****

"What happened to Millie?" I asked, as I rested in his arms later that night.

"She left a couple of weeks ago to start her own PR firm."

"Well, why'd you let her go?"

"I don't believe in holding people back, baby."

"Oh, I see."

"I think you'll like Lloyd. He's smart and he's excited about our partnership with your blog, thinks it's an ingenious idea."

I bet, since he rejected my proposal.

"We were really fortunate he was looking to make the move to Houston right now. He has some great ideas to further our marketing reach. He brings a lot to the table with his experience working at Adventure."

I nodded against his chest. I couldn't argue with any of that. Lloyd was smart and a hard worker. "I wonder what made him want to leave Adventure," I thought aloud.

"Why? You think Sable Jets is not reputable enough for someone like him?"

I raised my head and looked him in the eye. "No, of course not, but it's a huge leap to go from that company to Sable Jets."

"He said he wanted to make a fresh start, and he was excited about working for a black-owned company."

"Hmm..."

"Damn, you sure are curious about this guy. Should I be concerned?"

I sat up and flicked on the bedside lamp. "Derek, I think I need to tell you something about Lloyd Robinson."

With his eyes piercing mine, he said, "He's your ex?"

I literally gasped. "You already knew? What the hell kind of game are you trying to play? You hired my damn ex on purpose?" I stood and snatched on my panties.

Derek sat up straight. "Wait, Greer, wait! I only figured it out tonight."

"Right. You probably checked his social media before you hired him and saw my dumb ass in some of his pictures. I told you I don't like games, Derek. I told you—"

He jumped out of bed and rushed to me in all his naked glory, placed his hands on my arms, and said, "With all due respect, I'm the damn CEO. I don't check social media accounts. I don't do background checks or anything similar to that. I have people hired to do that. I put two and two together based on your reaction to seeing him, his reaction to seeing you, and his wife's reaction to both of you. Plus, she was wearing the same cheap-ass ring you had on when I first met you."

"My ring wasn't cheap."

"It was, baby. When I give you one, you'll see the difference. Now calm down and come back to bed."

"No."

"Why not?"

"Because...because I feel stupid."

"Don't. Just come back to bed."

I shook my head. "I can't work with him, Derek."

"I take it he cheated on you with Tami, got her pregnant in the process?"

I nodded as I let him lead me to the bed. "Then he broke up with me by blocking me on social media and replacing me with Tami as his fiancée unbeknownst to me."

"Shit..."

"I know. Look, I'm not mad. I never really was all that hurt. I love you and what we have together, Derek. I really do, but you can't blame me for not wanting to work with him."

He lay back in bed and pulled me to him. "No, I get it. I really do. I wouldn't want to work with any of my exes. I tell you what, I'll handle everything with your deal personally."

"No, I know you don't have time for that. You have other things to be concerned about."

"Nothing is more important to me than you. I'm angry about how he treated you, but I'm grateful at the same time. But for his stupidity, you wouldn't be mine. But look, if his working for Sable Jets is going to make trouble for us, I'll fire his ass in a heartbeat."

"No...if you're sure you can handle the extra work..."

"How many times do I have to tell you I'm the CEO? It's *my* company, named after *my* mother. I can always delegate something else to make room for your deal. Don't worry about me. I'm a big boy."

"Oh, I'm well aware of that."

"Is that right?"

"Yes, sir."

"You keep talking like that, you're gonna get something started."

"Hell, I hope so."

He rolled over, stretching his body over mine and kissing me deeply. "I love you, Greer Kennedy."

"I love you, too, Derek Hill."

28

Greer

"Ladies, that concludes the FaceTime tour of the Hill Mansion," I said, as I walked back into the living room and sat on the couch. Denise's and Trevia's smiling faces filled the screen of my phone.

"Girl, that's a nice house! No wonder you moved in with him," Trevia said.

"Hell, all those bedrooms up in there, I might be at your doorstep in a few minutes," Denise joked...or maybe she wasn't joking.

"I didn't technically move in here. I mean, all of my stuff is still in my apartment. I just kind of came with my one little suitcase and never left."

With pursed lips, Denise shook her head. "Umph! That is some kinda penis he got on him. Sheeeit, you were with Lloyd way longer than this and you never played house with him."

I grinned. "Number one, Lloyd is no Derek. Number two, he does have an excellent penis, a *superb* penis, an astronomical penis!"

Trevia clamped a hand over her mouth and let out a muffled laugh. "You are so crazy! That doesn't even make sense!"

"For real, it's so good, I'm sitting here tryna figure out how there wasn't already some woman up in here. These Houston heifers are slipping. And get this, his last girlfriend cheated on him!"

"Girl, as good as you say he is in bed, I'd be afraid to meet the man she cheated with," Denise said.

"Me, too!" I shouted. "Denise, how's my apartment doing?"

"It's fine. I've been going by there checking on it every day."

"Why don't you just stay there for now? Make things easier for yourself."

"For real? Oh, thank you! I'm about one click from strangling my mama! You saved me from getting arrested."

I chuckled. "No problem at all. It's been sitting there unoccupied for three weeks now, and the lease won't be up for another few months."

"What do I owe you? I can't afford much, but I'm willing to pay."

"Don't worry about it right now. Just get your credit together so you can eventually take over the lease for me."

"I sure will! Well, we'll let you go. I know you're supposed to be meeting Mr. Hill for lunch," Denise said.

"Wait!" Trevia yelled. "You've been in a relationship with this man for months and now you're living with him. When do we get to meet him?"

"Yeah! Shit, hop on one of those jets and come get us," Denise added.

"It's not a car, 'Nise. But I'll find a way to introduce you guys to him. You're gonna love him!"

With a dreamy look on her face, Trevia said, "As happy as he's making you, we already do."

I exited the car Derek sent for me and appraised my appearance in the mirrored side of the building before entering it. I smiled at the fit of my black pencil skirt and red silk tank under a black leather jacket. We were having lunch in Derek's office, and with any luck, my skirt would be rolled up around my waist before the end of the date.

I rubbed my hand over my waist-length box braids and finally entered the building, snaking my way through the crowd of people in the lobby to the elevator bank. As I stood with several other people waiting for an elevator, a text message came through.

It was from Derek: *I'm waiting for u and I hope ur sexy ass is wearing a skirt.*

Me: *A skirt and no panties.*

Derek: *Aw, shit!!!!!! Hurry up and get here!*

Me: *Getting on the elevator now.*

Phone in hand, I stepped into the elevator with a huge smile on my face. I couldn't wait to see my man. I waited as the elevator filled with bodies and dropped my smile when Tami, who looked like she was exactly one second from exploding, boarded and stood near the doors. She glanced toward the back where I stood and gave me a little smile. I frowned.

We both got off on the same floor, of course, and headed toward the offices of Sable Inc., Tami a few paces ahead of me. Imagine my surprise when she stopped in her tracks down the hall from the office and faced me. "I want to ask you a favor," she said, giving me some weird-ass sincere look.

I glanced around at the empty hallway. "A favor? You don't even know me."

"I know *of* you. Lloyd has nothing but really good things to say about you."

I tilted my neck back and scoffed. "Am I supposed to be excited about Lloyd's opinion of me?"

"No, it's just that I need your help with something for him, and I thought you'd be more willing if you understood neither he nor I hold any malice for you."

Was this bitch out of her mind? "Malice? Are you insane?" I stepped around her and continued toward the office.

"Wait! If I apologize for sleeping with Lloyd while you were with him will you at least hear me out?"

I turned back around and moved closer to her. "Maybe, but make it quick. My man, your husband's boss, is waiting to bend me over his desk and screw my brains out."

She blinked hard. "Oh...well, I'm sorry for sleeping with Lloyd while the two of you were together. It was wrong, but we just happened to fall in love."

"Mm-hmm..."

"And I wanted to ask if maybe you could stop flaunting your relationship with Mr. Hill in front of Lloyd. He's having a hard time concentrating on his job, because he says you're always there meeting with Mr. Hill. He's sure you were seeing him before you two broke up."

"Do I look like I give any variable amount of damns about that? He can think what he wants."

"Well, he's thinking about quitting, and I've already let him uproot me once because of you." There was an edge to her voice.

"What the hell are you talking about?"

"He felt so guilty about how things worked out with you, he decided to leave Dallas, and then he gets here and runs into you again and you're with the CEO. It's been hard for him to cope with."

I just stood there and stared at her. How could I respond to this craziness? Was she actually trying to blame me for what they did?

"We can't move again. Not right now. We're about to have a baby."

She sounded so serious, so sincere, I almost didn't say what I said. *Almost.*

I chuckled lightly. "Soooo, you're standing here telling me your *husband* is jealous of me and my man? You know how pathetic you sound?"

"I—"

"Look, I'm not going to stop doing shit to spare Lloyd's feelings. He's your problem now. Not mine. Now you have a nice day, a nice week, hell, a nice life, but don't come at me with this stupidity ever again."

I turned to leave then stopped and faced her again. "If you had asked, I would've told you Lloyd ain't shit. Now you know, don't you?"

A few seconds later, I entered the main office, waved at the receptionist, and headed straight to Derek's office, passing Lloyd's office and flashing him a dazzling smile on my way there. I knocked and let myself into Derek's office where he greeted me with a smile and a tight embrace. I eyed the food set up on a table in the corner of the room and whispered, "Close the blinds, baby."

He backed away a little and with a grin, said, "You want dessert first, huh?"

I bit my bottom lip and nodded.

After he hurriedly locked the door and closed the blinds on the windows that gave him a view of the cubicles, I pulled my skirt up around my waist, bent over the desk, and sang, "Come and get it."

29

Greer

A trip to Vail, Colorado, sounded like a good idea, especially since it was January and it was miserably cold in Texas, miserably cold without the benefit of the gorgeous snowy landscape characteristic of Vail. So when I took a poll of my followers to find out where they wanted me to visit next, I was both shocked and happy to oblige them by traveling to the winter wonderland. When I invited Derek and he agreed to accompany me, the idea of going there went from good to excellent. So I began researching the area as I always did before a trip, and came up with an itinerary for our three-day vacation. But, the day before we were to leave, he backed out. I made all these plans for us, and he gave me some business-related excuse at the last minute. And, no, our black asses weren't hitting the slopes or anything like that, but there were plans and now I'd have to do all that shit alone.

And I was pissed at him.

Very pissed.

So pissed that when he kissed me goodbye the morning of my departure and told me to have fun, I rolled my eyes. I stalked around the house for an hour after he left for work, didn't even call him as I usually would when I boarded the jet. The crazy thing is, I don't know why I was so mad at him. It wasn't as if I wasn't accustomed to traveling alone. In all the years I'd been a travel blogger, even before it became a full-time gig for me, I almost always traveled alone except for a few times when Denise or Trevia or both of them tagged along and the very rare occasion Lloyd accompanied me. For the most part, I loved traveling alone. Sure, there were times I wished someone I cared for could experience certain things with me, but I'd never felt so despondent about traveling alone before. I suppose it was the thought of being separated from Derek that bothered me more than anything. I just didn't want to be away from him. Not then. Not ever.

Because I loved him.

Really and truly I did. He was my first real love. Not Lloyd Robinson or anyone else. Just Derek Dwight Hill.

I reclined in the soft leather seat and gazed out the window at the sky and the clouds and wished I was in his arms right that moment.

*****

The lodge in Vail was warm and homey and cozy, decorated in shades of brown with a rustic feel to it. It was one of the top-rated lodging establishments in the area, and a Sable Jets affiliate. I had the presence of mind to take photos of the exterior and the interior common areas, but the thrill I usually felt when I traveled was gone. Shit, Derek Hill had tamed my ass for real, had me wishing I was on his couch waiting for him to get home from work.

So I spent my first day in Vail pouting in my room. Damn near jumped for joy when Derek called me that evening. I was equal parts mad at him and elated to hear his voice.

"So how was day one? You get some good pictures for your blog?"

"A few..."

"A few? I thought the itinerary you made was packed with stuff."

"It is. I just didn't feel like doing any of it today, so I stayed in my room."

"Stayed in your room? What's wrong?"

"Nothing."

"You sick?"

"No, I'm not sick."

"Then what is it?"

"I told you. Nothing."

"Greer, come on. Tell me what's wrong."

"You know what's wrong. I wanted you to come with me. You're supposed to be here. Not there. I'm lonely."

"I'm sorry."

"I miss you."

"You know I miss you, too. I'll make it up to you. I promise."

"If you say so..."

"You ever known me to lie to you?"

I sighed. "No."

"Then you know I'll make it up to you. I had to stay here and work. It couldn't be avoided, baby."

"What happened to all that big bad 'I'm the CEO' stuff?"

"Even the CEO has to work from time to time. Hey, promise me you'll go out and do some stuff tomorrow. I'm making this request not only as your man but as your business associate. The Nubian Nomad is your baby. Don't let your readers or Sable Jets down because I messed up."

"You didn't mess up. You had to work. That's what grown-ups do."

"So you forgive me?"

"Yes, but when I get home on Sunday you better be waiting for me butt-ass naked."

"Hell, I already planned to do that. I love you. Enjoy yourself, okay?"

"I love you, too. I'll try."

*****

The next morning, Derek called and gave me a little pep talk encouraging me to seize the day and do all I could to bring Vail to my readers. So after a huge breakfast, I dressed in some of the warm, expensive clothes I bought specially for the trip and ventured into town, where I lost track of time shopping and eating and taking tons of pictures. I even tweeted and Instagrammed a bunch of them, and I sent Derek a video of me having lunch. By dinner time, I was exhausted and had decided to forgo eating and just collapse into bed. I entered the lodge with shopping bags in both hands, my mind so preoccupied with the idea of getting some rest that I ran right into someone. "Oh, excuse me. I'm sorry," I said, only giving them half a glance.

"You good, girl."

I stopped and looked at the woman. I'd know her voice anywhere. "Denise?!" I shrieked, as I dropped the bags and threw my arms around her. "What are you doing here?"

She giggled and backed away a bit. "What are any of us doing here?"

With a deeply furrowed brow, I asked, "What?" I looked around and almost instantly pressed my hand to my mouth. Lit candles occupied every surface in the huge, living room-like lobby. Five or six people were standing around me, all dressed in white. In the dimness, I had to really focus before recognizing Trevia and Derek's brother and sister-in-law. Hell, even Millie was there. Then I turned and behind me saw a sight that made me gasp. "Mama? Daddy?"

I rushed to my smiling parents and hugged them both at the same time. They were dressed in white, too. "What's going on?" I asked through tears. "Why are y'all here?"

"I invited them. I invited everyone."

Derek.

His voice came from somewhere behind me. I was afraid that if I turned to face him, I'd lose it. So I didn't.

His voice grew closer as he continued speaking. "I wanted this to be special. I wanted to be sure everyone we knew and loved, those that are closest to us, were here for this."

Tears poured from my eyes as my parents smiled at me. I felt a hand on my shoulder, heard Derek say, "I flew them all here for you. For us."

I sniffled. "That's why you wanted me to leave the lodge today?"

"Yes."

I smiled and shook my head but didn't and couldn't face him yet.

"Greer, when I met you all those months ago, I knew you were beautiful, smart, fearless, fiery, and more than a little mysterious. What I didn't know was that you held the key to my heart inside of you."

I was blubbering like an idiot. I mean, I had Kim Kardashian beat with my ugly cry.

He reached for my hand and spun me around to face him. Dressed in a crisp white Mandarin collar shirt and white slacks with his dreadlocks pulled into a neat ponytail at the back of his head, he looked like everything I'd ever dreamed of, my king.

He lowered himself onto one knee, and I tightly shut my eyes and told myself to stop crying. Myself didn't listen.

"Open your eyes, baby," he softly said.

I did, and almost fell backward at the sight of the ring he held. It made Lloyd's ring look like it came from the dollar store.

"Greer Charlene Kennedy, I love you with all my heart and soul. You are everything to me, and I want to spend the rest of my life making you as happy as you've made me. I want to see the world with you, have kids with you, grow old with you. Greer, will you marry me?"

I swiped at my wet eyes and sighed. "Y-yes. Yes, I will. I love you so much."

He slid the ring onto my finger, stood, and pulled me to him. I wrapped my arms around him and cried tears of joy until I could cry no more.

30

Derek

Lying on my back with Greer's naked body straddling mine, I smiled, happy that my plan had all worked out. A million things could've gone wrong. Greer could have returned to the lodge before we were ready, or someone could've backed out of coming, or she could've said no. Anything. But as it stood, everything worked out, and the woman peering down at me was now my fiancée.

"You made me cry. Not just cry, but *ugly* cry," she said.

"I didn't mean to, but they were tears of joy, right?"

"Absolutely. But how did you pull this off? How'd you get in touch with Trevia and Denise and my parents? You'd never even met any of them before now, right?"

"You don't have a password or lock code on your phone. All I had to do was knock you out with some sex and snoop and get the numbers."

She threw her head back and laughed. "Is that right? You think you be knocking me out?"

I raised an eyebrow. "You saying I don't? Am I gonna have to prove myself?"

"No, baby. I was just playing. You know you be putting me in comas on the regular."

I reached up and pulled her down onto my chest. "Naw, don't get scared now."

"I'm not scared, just tired, exhausted. And...thank you."

I rubbed her back and gently kissed her lips. "For what?"

"For being a real man and showing me real love. And...for proving that Lloyd's ring *was* cheap."

I grinned. "I told your ass. I love you, Greer. I don't think you have any idea how much."

"Can't be as much as I love you." She kissed me, sat up, and reached down between us, grabbing hold of my manhood which sprung to attention, as it always did for her.

Looking into her eyes, I said, "I thought you were tired."

"I am," she replied, as she guided me inside of her. "I want you to put me in one of those comas."

I grabbed her hips and sucked in a breath. "You got it, baby."

*****

On the flight back home, Greer set us up some joint social media accounts since I didn't have any (just wasn't my thing) so I could reconnect with some of my old friends and invite them to the wedding that I wanted to have sooner rather than later. But I knew it would take time to plan everything, and I wanted her to have whatever she wanted—big or small. All I knew was I felt like the luckiest man on earth to have found this woman where I did when I did. I was feeling so good, I seriously considered giving Lloyd Robinson a raise. Stevie

Wonder could look at him and sense his misery. He messed up, and he knew it, but to my advantage. Any man who would let go of a woman like Greer was a damn fool, and I wasn't going to ever let that happen to me. She was mine, and I was hers.

Forever.

31

Greer

We weren't doing shit.

I mean, we were doing absolutely nothing...and I loved it. I loved just sitting in his living room wearing an old pair of jeans and my favorite t-shirt, reading a book while he sat right next to me on his laptop reading something on some business website. He was wearing sweats and a t-shirt. No underwear because I could tell, and my mouth watered every time I glanced in his direction. I was content to be there in that big room with its manly but cozy decor. Very content.

I felt with him the same way I felt when I first started traveling, like I had discovered some hidden part of myself. It was kind of like learning a new skill. The person is whole to begin with, but with the new skill, they are an enhanced version of who they already were. Derek didn't necessarily complete me, because I was already a fully-actualized woman before I knew him. I understood who I was and what my place was in the world. I was fully aware of what I liked and disliked. I knew where I was in my career and where I was trying to go. Connecting my life to Derek's enhanced me, gave me someone to share myself with on every level. And while he enhanced me, I complemented him, gave him someone he could be himself with, made it okay for him to be both the Derek I met in Virginia and the Texas CEO at the same time.

"Why're you staring at me?" he asked, closing the laptop and giving me his attention.

"I'm tryna figure out how you could possibly look that good in sweats and a t-shirt. You know you're fine, right? I mean, you have been told that once or twice before?"

He shrugged as he reached over and squeezed my thigh. "I think it was just once."

"You're such a liar."

"Okay, twice."

I rolled my eyes.

He glanced at his watch. "Hmm, it's almost noon. What do you want to do today?"

"Honestly, I wanna sit right here and chill with you. Maybe watch a movie or something on TV or Netflix."

"Is that right? What about lunch? Want me to run out and grab something?"

I shook my head. "I can fix us something. You're getting a full-service woman here. I cook, I clean. Okay, I clean *sometimes*. I—"

"You put it on me in the bedroom..."

I giggled. "You're so crazy!"

With a big, cheesy grin on his face, he said, "You do. How do you think you got that ring?"

"I better have it because you love me!"

"I do love you, baby. I also love it when you put it on me."

"Wow, and all this time I thought you wanted me for my brain, my beauty…"

"I do…and your booty."

I swatted at him and he grabbed my arm, pulling me to him. "You know I love the hell out of you, right?"

"I do. You know I love *you*, right?"

"Yeah, and seriously, baby, I love you because you're real. You're real enough to curse me out if you need to, you're real enough to have my back when I need it, and you're real enough to walk the red carpet one day and sit here and be bored with me the next and not complain."

"I could never be bored as long as you're wearing those pants."

He chuckled as he leaned in and pressed his lips to the hollow of my neck. "Really, baby? That's all it takes to entertain you?"

"Yep. A pair of jogging pants sans underwear will do it. It's like watching a pendulum swing on a big, humongous-ass grandfather clock."

He threw his head back and laughed while I climbed into his lap, wrapped my arms around his neck, and asked, "You know why I love you?"

"Because of my pendulum?"

"Damn, you guessed it."

He gave me a smirk.

I smiled and kissed his cheek. "I love you because you're brilliant, you can run a boardroom and then come home and run the hell out of our bedroom with your nasty ass."

He lifted a brow. "Am I nasty, baby?"

"Hell yes, and you're also kind, you treat me like a queen, and you are sexy all at the same time."

"Girl, you keep talking like that and you're gonna get yourself in some trouble up in here."

"Mm-hmm, so what do you want for lunch, Mr. CEO?"

He looked me dead in the eye, and said, "You."

I adjusted myself so that I was straddling him. "Well, tic toc, baby."

32

Greer

I wasn't sure at first what pulled me out of a sound sleep, but when I rolled over and reached for Derek, finding his side of the bed empty, I realized it was the absence of his warmth that had awakened me. I shifted my eyes to the bathroom door to find it ajar and the bathroom dark. Sitting up, I frowned slightly, glanced at the clock that sat on the nightstand on Derek's side of the bed to see that it was only 2:00 AM. I climbed out of bed, wrapping the sheet around my naked body, and drowsily walked through the huge house. I finally found Derek sitting at the kitchen table on his laptop.

He looked up and sighed. "You're up? I tried my best not to disturb you. Sorry, baby."

I approached him, stepped behind his chair, and leaned in to get a look at the screen. "Work?"

He glanced up at me. "Yeah. Got a meeting first thing in the morning. Reading over this contract trying to figure out what's missing."

As I took a seat across from him, he rubbed his hands over his face and closed his eyes.

"You need rest," I said. "Come back to bed for a couple of hours.

Wake up with fresh eyes and look at it again."

"Yeah...I should do that," he said absently, fixing his eyes back on the screen.

"Derek, you're working too hard. I know this new deal is important to you, but you're going to wear yourself out."

He nodded, his attention still on the computer. "I know."

I watched him for five minutes before leaving my seat and dropping the sheet. I walked over to him and said, "Scoot back."

He looked up at me with tired eyes that brightened a bit when he noticed I was now exposed, and complied with my request. I slid into his lap and licked his bottom lip before kissing him deeply. "Come back to bed, and I will make it worth your while."

He wrapped his arms around me. "You're playing dirty. How the hell am I supposed to refuse that offer?"

*****

"Hey, my boy Christian is gonna be by this morning. He wants to look at my Mercedes."

I bent over and checked my muffins in the oven. "Okay. You still sure you want to sell it?"

"Yeah, I haven't driven it in years, and you say you don't want it, so we don't need it."

"Okay, if you're sure..."

"I am. Just let him in the garage when he gets there."

"All right."

"You got any plans for today?"

I perched on a kitchen stool and sighed. "Not too many. Someone had me up late last night."

"You started that. I was minding my own business, working."

"You were being a workaholic. I offered you the balance you needed."

"You sure did. You always do, and I love you for it. So you're taking it easy today?"

"For the most part. I just need to work on finalizing plans for the Essence Festival, see if my blog can get me some media passes. Cross your fingers for me."

"Fingers and toes crossed, baby. I have a lunch meeting so I won't see you until this evening. Love you."

"Love you, too."

I set my phone on the counter and sighed again. I had spent the month since our engagement obsessing over planning the wedding, and it had stressed me out to the point that Derek begged me to let him hire a wedding planner. I just didn't want to do that. I wanted to plan out every detail myself. I wanted our day to be personal and magical, but even I had to admit I was overwhelmed. Yeah, I planned out my trips myself, but by and large I was not a planner. At least not when it came to something as big as a wedding. The major things in my life sort of just happened—becoming a travel blogger, meeting Derek, hell, even meeting Lloyd. So we agreed to hold off on the planning. As Derek said, we were in no rush. Neither of us were going anywhere. I sure as hell wasn't. He was stuck with me.

An hour later, Derek's friend, Christian, arrived to check out the Mercedes that, as far as I could tell, was in mint condition. Derek had told me it was the first vehicle he bought for himself after he and his brother took over operations of Sable Inc. and that it sort of symbolized his transition into both business and official manhood. He said he could let it go now, because he was making another transition with me. Plus, he owned two other vehicles and most days preferred being driven to work via a car service.

After Christian checked the car out, I invited him in for something to drink. He was tall, handsome, about Derek's complexion with a bald head. I had learned from Derek that he owned a car lot, hence his interest in the Mercedes. I also knew he was single, and I thought he and Trevia would make a good match, not that I thought for a second she would leave sorry-ass Wesley alone.

"Derek said you've known each other since high school?" I asked, as we sat at the kitchen table, me sipping coffee and Christian drinking water.

He nodded. "Yeah, we've always been pretty close. We were on the basketball team together, warming the bench. We sucked!"

I laughed. "He failed to mention that to me."

"I bet he did. Hey, I'm surprised it took him so long to let us meet, but I guess he wanted to be sure this time."

"This time?"

"Yeah, you know about Sasha, right? His last girlfriend? Gold digger extraordinaire?"

"Oh, her," I said through a chuckle. "He said she was something else."

"She was. He introduced her to me and our other friends pretty quickly, but I never did see them as a match. Derek likes to spoil his lady because that's the way his pops treated his mom. Sasha took advantage of that. I knew they weren't going to work out. I really think Derek was looking for something he didn't find until you. Glad you two got together. He's happier than I've ever seen him. He's a good man, Greer."

"That he definitely is. I'm happy to be with him."

"Good. Seeing what you two have gives me hope."

I smiled. "You looking to settle down?"

"Absolutely. I'd love to get married and have some kids. Got any single friends?" He laughed after making that statement, but I knew he was at least partially serious.

"I'll keep my eyes and ears open for you."

"I'd appreciate that."

About five minutes after Christian left, the doorbell rang again. I glanced at the kitchen table to see if he'd left something behind, but all I saw were our cups. Then I thought maybe he left something in the garage. I opened the door without benefit of checking the peep hole, and said, "Did you forget something?" before realizing it wasn't Christian at the door, but a woman. A very pretty woman with flawless dark skin, full lips, blond hair, and a huge belly.

"Oh, I'm sorry. I thought you were someone else. Um, can I help you?"

She shook her head and dug in the black and white, chevron-patterned purse that hung from her shoulder, unearthing a piece of paper, a check, and thrusting it in my face. It was a check Derek had written for fifty thousand dollars. It was endorsed to one Sasha Porter.

"No," she said, "but *I* can help *you*."

33

Derek

My house was dark and empty when I finally made it home much later than anticipated. I'd been calling Greer all afternoon and evening, trying to see if she would have dinner with me in my office, but she never answered. I left several messages and texted her at least ten times. Still no answer. So I left the office with a heavy heart. She was pissed about something. Maybe about how much I'd been working lately, but I thought she understood Sable Inc. was acquiring a new company and that kind of thing requires my close attention. She said she understood, but maybe she didn't. Or maybe she was just tired of sitting in my house by herself.

The house was so quiet, it almost felt as cold as it did before she moved in—cold and lonely. I slowly ascended the stairs, a feeling of doom floating around me like fog. Alarms were going off in my head. It was too damn quiet. An empty kind of quiet. I knew before I reached our bedroom that she wasn't there. But what I didn't expect was to find her portion of the closet empty or to see her perfume no longer on the dresser or to find her ring sitting on the bedside table.

I dropped my briefcase on the floor and slumped onto the bed and sat there wondering what happened. What had gone wrong? How had I missed whatever signs there were that pointed to this happening? To her leaving me?

Shit, how did I mess this up? Or was it me?

I glanced around the room, looking for what? A clue? An explanation?

Damn, what am I supposed to do now?

I dialed her number again—straight to voicemail. I thought about calling one of her friends, but knew they would probably ignore me, too.

I've got to do something. I've got to get her back.

I snatched the ring from the table and at that moment, noticed the piece of paper it had been sitting on. A check.

I picked it up, and when I saw exactly what check it was, I knew what had happened.

Sasha was here.

34

Greer

I was in my bedroom, in my apartment, digging into a whole gallon of ice cream that evening when Denise made it back. I had finally stopped crying, or maybe I had just grown too exhausted to cry. After Sasha's little visit that morning, I had packed my things and was on the first plane back home in less than two hours. My heart was aching so badly, I now fully understood the term broken heart, but my heart had nothing on my head. It felt like it was about to split in two.

Thoughts of the pretty pregnant woman's words filled my mind as I looked down at the rapidly melting ice cream I'd barely tasted. I had no appetite, no desire to do anything but sit and think and overthink. How did things go so wrong? What was with me and choosing men? What was with me and accepting marriage proposals from assholes?

Maybe I was constantly forcing something that was just not meant to be for me. Maybe I was meant to work alone, travel alone, live alone...be alone. Otherwise, things with men wouldn't always end like this—with another woman and a baby.

Shit. Another damn baby.

What. The. Hell?

"Hey, I'm back!" Denise announced, as she walked into the

bedroom with a paper sack.

"Hey," I said. "I'm sorry again for popping up like this."

"Girl, it's your apartment. I can sleep on the couch or go back to my mom's. No biggie. I just want you to be all right."

"Then erase the last few years of my life or give me amnesia so I won't remember these two shitty engagements or the bastards who gave me the rings."

"Well, I can't do that, sis. But I do have pie." She pulled what I recognized as one of her mother's pies from the sack and flashed me a smile.

I laughed despite my pain. "You stole another pie?"

"No, I actually took this one right in front of her, told her it was an emergency situation."

"And she accepted that?"

"No, she made me elaborate. Girl, when I told her you and your fine, rich, CEO boyfriend had broken up, she not only let me take the pie, but she gave me this." She reached back into the sack and pulled out a canister of whipped cream this time.

I laughed lightly while shaking my head. It didn't take long for the laughter to flow into tears. I was a damn emotional wreck.

"Where the hell is Trevia?" Denise ranted. "I don't know how to handle you when you're like this. You barely ever get emotional. You usually just go with the flow and be all que sera, sera and shit. I swear I'ma curse her ass out. She's supposed to be here!" She sat down next to me and snatched me into a hug.

I relaxed against her and through sobs, said, "I love him, 'Nise. I love him so much. What am I supposed to do now?"

"Well, maybe you should talk to him. You just up and left and didn't get his side."

I sat up and wiped my eyes. "He gave her a check for fifty thousand dollars. She says he tried to pay her to abort his baby. He kicked her out of his house a couple of weeks before I pretty much moved in. What kind of man does that?"

"That just doesn't sound like Derek, Greer."

"You don't even know him!"

"I know enough. He's a good man, and he definitely loves you. You've got to at least hear his side."

"He's not gonna tell the truth. He tried to make her out to just be an ex, never mentioned a baby at all."

"Greer, maybe...never mind."

"What?"

"Maybe this is more about what Lloyd did than Derek."

"No, it's about Derek lying to me and trying to pay off a pregnant woman. I saw the check, held it in my hands. It was his sloppy-ass handwriting and it was dated within the time frame of us being together. Why would he give her that much money and not tell me if everything was on the up and up?"

"I don't know."

"Neither do I."

A knock at the door startled me so badly, I dropped the now soupy ice cream on the floor. "Shit!" I yelled.

"I'll clean it up," Denise offered. "That's probably Trevia. Can you let her in?"

I nodded. "I'm surprised she didn't use her key." Dressed in a ratty t-shirt and bleach-splattered jogging pants, I dragged myself to the door. "Why didn't you use your key?" I asked through the door before opening it to reveal Derek.

Derek

She moved to close the door in my face, but I grabbed it before she could. "Baby, I need to talk to you," I said. Her eyes were red and puffy, and there was a look of sadness in them that broke my heart. I had never laid a hand on a woman in my life before, but right that second I really wanted to put my foot in Sasha's ass.

Greer shook her pretty head. "No, go away."

"I can't do that. I need you to hear me out. I need to tell you the truth, because I know Sasha didn't."

"No, just leave, Derek. Please leave. Move so I can close this door."

"No."

"I'll call the police."

"No you won't. You're upset. You deserve to be upset with me, but you also love me. You don't want me arrested. Let me in, baby. Let me explain."

She dropped her eyes and shook her head.

"If you don't let me in, I'm going to sit at your doorstep until you do. I don't care if I have to sit out here for a year. Let me in, *please*."

She sighed and moved to the side, allowing me into the apartment. Her friend, Denise, walked into the living room and gave me a surprised look. "Uh…I'ma go see what's going on with Trevia. Be right back."

As she breezed past both of us, Greer said, "Wait!" But Denise was already gone.

"Can we sit?" I asked.

"No. Just say what you've got to say and leave."

"Okay, what did Sasha tell you?"

"What do you think? She told me a whole bunch of shit that seemed to slip your mind."

"She told you she's pregnant with my child?"

"Yep."

"Why'd she say I gave her the check?"

"To get rid of her and the baby."

"Well, that's partially true, the part about getting rid of her at least."

"She said she was living with you shortly before I moved in."

"No, she was living in my house. I wasn't living there at the time."

"Even if that's true, and I don't believe a word you're saying, but if it *is* true, you still kept it from me."

"Okay, I acknowledge I was wrong for not telling you what was going on with her, but I didn't think it was important. *She* wasn't important. Hell, she's still not."

She scoffed and shook her head. "Now why the hell would I want a man who thinks the mother of his child is not important?"

"She's not the mother of my child. She's not the mother of *any* child! She's not even pregnant!"

35

Derek

"Oh, come on! Are you serious? I saw her *and* her big-ass stomach, Derek! Try again!" Greer shouted.

"It's a prosthesis or something. Like those outfits guys wear to know what it feels like to be pregnant."

She took a seat on her sofa and buried her face in her hands. "You are really a piece of shit. An unimaginative piece of shit. How could I fall in love with you?"

"Because you know what kind of man I am. I'm telling the truth, and Sasha is crazy as hell. Look, her house burned down after we broke up, and she called asking if she could crash at my place because she doesn't have any family in the state. I told her sure. This was a few weeks before I met you. So she arrived at my place and I honestly thought she'd just gained some weight until she told me she was pregnant with my baby.

"Greer, baby, I didn't believe it from day one. After all, I knew she'd been with someone else and I always used protection. Always. Hell, I'm not dumb. So I told her I wanted a DNA test. She started crying, talking about how on top of losing her home she'd lost her job, so I let it go and decided to bring it up later. I felt kind of sorry for her."

She looked up at me and sighed. "You say you weren't living at your house when she was there. Where were you staying?"

"In my office mostly. Sometimes I'd get a room."

"So you didn't screw her while she was there? Not once?"

"Hell no! Sasha and I were over long before I even met you. Shit, we were over before we were over."

"What difference does that make? We weren't a couple in Virginia and you screwed the hell out of me."

"Sasha is not you. Not by a long shot."

She dropped her eyes again. "What about the money?"

"I offered it as an incentive for her to take the paternity test, and it worked because all she's ever cared about is my money. We went to the clinic together. When they called me back, they told me she wasn't even pregnant. She was in the doctor's office crying, saying all this crazy shit about how much she loved me and would do anything to be with me. She'd taken that fake stomach off, and it was lying on a chair next to her. Greer, I was in shock. I mean, I knew she could be manipulative, but this was past that. Sasha is mentally ill."

I walked over to her, squatted in front of her, placed my hands on her knees, and said, "I made her move out that day. I don't know where she went, but I told her to take the check and cash it and check herself into a psychiatric center. She needs help."

She didn't speak or look up at me.

"Baby, you've got to believe me. I'm telling you the truth. Sasha is not pregnant. She's crazy, and she's just trying to make my life miserable. I don't know how she even knows about you."

"Facebook."

"What?"

"She says she saw a picture of us on Facebook. That damn Facebook just keeps ruining my relationships."

"No, not this time. Not if you believe me. I love you and I am not lying."

She finally looked me in the eye. "But you did lie...by omission. She was living in your house, and you never told me. You said you had no kids when you weren't even sure of it. You kept me in the dark on purpose."

"Because I didn't want to lose you. And I'm so sorry for that."

"So am I. If you'd just told me, maybe..."

"Maybe what?"

"Maybe we could be together. Maybe I'd believe you. Right now I don't know what to believe."

I clutched my chest. "Believe me, baby. I messed up. I see that now, but I'm telling the truth."

"How can I believe you, Derek?"

"I know I still got your heart. Your heart believes in me. Trust it."

As tears rolled down her cheeks, she said, "I can't. I'm tired of being made a fool of."

"Please, Greer don't do this. Don't let her do this to us."

"*You* did this, Derek. You should've been up front with me about everything. Now please just go."

"Greer—"

She pushed against me, almost knocking me to the floor as she sprung to her feet. "Go! Get out! Get the fuck outta my house now!"

I stood and approached her cautiously. "Baby, please..."

"Out! Now!"

"Baby, please. You know I love you. I'd do anything for you. You know that."

"Anything including paying off your baby's mother?"

"She's not pregnant! I'm telling you, she's not!"

"I don't believe you! Get out of here now!"

I squeezed my eyes shut and realized there was no use, at least not right now. So I left, and she slammed the door behind me so hard I was surprised it didn't break.

Once inside my rental car, I pounded my fist against the steering wheel. "Fuck!"

36

Greer

Derek Hill possessed a level of persistence I had never witnessed before, and I honestly didn't know how to fight it. When he wasn't calling, he was texting. When he wasn't texting, he was emailing. Flowers were delivered to my apartment nearly every waking hour of the day. My place looked like either a florist or a wedding chapel. It had been two weeks since I left him, and I was no closer to getting over him than day one, because he was always present in some form. I suppose that was his strategy—to overwhelm me with these gestures. He was succeeding.

This was CEO Derek, a calculated, relentless strategist—the man behind the success of Sable Inc. This was the same man who kept Lloyd on for the benefit of the company despite the fact that he didn't like him as a person and who saw Lloyd's treatment of me as his good fortune. This was bottom-line Derek Hill, and the bottom line was he wanted me back, and just like anything he set his mind to, he wasn't giving up until he attained his goal.

And his goal was me.

And I wanted him to win this contest for my heart as much as he did.

That was the sad part. As badly as I wanted to be angry at his persistence or annoyed by the attention, I couldn't be. I wanted to be convinced I'd made a mistake. I wanted to see irrefutable evidence of his innocence.

Because I loved him.

And I missed him.

And I was totally and completely miserable without him. I wanted to believe him. I wanted that more than I had ever wanted anything in my entire life. But how could I? How could I believe him? What woman in her right mind would believe that someone, and someone as attractive as Sasha, would go to the extremes he claimed she had to...to what? I wasn't even sure what her purpose in all this was supposed to be. To trap him? Put him on child support? Get him to marry her? It just didn't make sense, and in my mind, senseless things were usually far from being true. Weren't they?

He sent a different type of flower every day. Today it was tulips—huge, gorgeous bouquets of tulips in multiple colors, all with cards attached which held the same message:

I love you. I'm sorry.

I sighed as I closed my eyes and rested my head on the back of my couch. I hadn't blogged or even been on the Internet except to watch Netflix. All I'd been doing was sitting around here staring and crying and wishing I never met Sasha Porter, and when I wasn't wishing that, I was wishing I'd never met Derek Hill.

The buzzing of my phone pulled my attention away from my sorrow for only a second, as I realized it was probably Derek calling. The sensible thing to do would be to change my number so he wouldn't be able to call anymore, but then he wouldn't be able to call anymore. If he couldn't call, he couldn't leave anymore voicemails. No more voicemails and I wouldn't be able to hear his voice.

I needed to hear his voice.

To my surprise it was Denise, who had moved back in with her mother because my apartment was just too small to share comfortably. "Hello?" I answered.

"Hey, I know you're not feeling all that well, but I need your help."

"What is it? Did you hit your mom?"

"No, not yet. It's Trevia. I need you to come help me calm her down. She's got a gun and is threatening to shoot Wesley."

*****

Trevia lived in a nice house in a nice neighborhood, a house the grandfather who raised her left her after he passed. Trevia also drove a nice car and made good money from her boutique. She was smart, money-savvy, and beautiful, so why she kept risking her freedom over a bum like Wesley was beyond me. Yes, he was fine, and from what I saw at the fated strip show where all three of us met him, he was super well-endowed, and I had no doubt he was skilled in bed. But damn, this relationship was a train wreck and she knew it. Just how much aggravation and humiliation was she willing to take to be with this man?

I walked up to her front door and knocked. Denise answered it with a disgusted look on her face. "You two bitches are gonna kill me with your relationship drama."

With a deep frown, I asked, "What's going on?"

"Hell, come in and see for yourself."

I followed Denise through Trevia's foyer into her spacious, all-white living room to find Trevia sitting on the couch looking…well, like a wild woman. She was hugging herself and rocking back and forth. Her huge afro was unkempt and she was wearing a wrap-style dress that hung so loosely from her it resembled a cheap robe, and Trevia didn't do cheap. Ever. She'd obviously lost quite a bit of weight in the weeks she'd gone MIA on us again. What on earth was going on? What the shit had Wesley done this time?

"Trevia?" I said softly, as I cautiously approached her and took a seat beside her. "Trevia, you okay?"

"Hell naw she ain't okay! Can't you see that?" Denise yelled. She was pacing in front of Trevia's white brick fireplace.

I shot Denise a look.

"What?" Denise asked, stopping in her tracks with both of her hands upturned.

I sighed and noticed the hot pink gun on the coffee table. "Will one of you tell me why there's a Hello Kitty-ass gun sitting here? Trevia, what were you planning to do with it?"

Trevia just kept rocking back and forth, and she was beginning to scare me. We'd all seen each other through some wild things, but I'd never seen her like this.

I looked up at Denise with raised eyebrows. "How did you know she was like this?"

"You know I've been trying to get in touch with her. I held off on using my key because I didn't want to walk in on something, but today I decided to take that chance. This heifer was headed out the door, gun in hand, ranting about, and I quote: 'Popping a cap in Wesley and that grimy bitch's ass.' Now, I don't know who said grimy bitch is, but I'm sure Sherlocka Homegirl here done dug up some stuff she can't handle, and I knew I needed some reinforcements if I was going to talk her off the ledge. I was barely able to get her back into the house. Bitch swung at me."

If Trevia called the woman a bitch, then this was definitely serious. Denise and I were the main cursers in our group. Not that Trevia didn't curse, but for her to use the word bitch? Well, she reserved usage of that word for highly stressful occasions.

"Okay..." I turned back to Trevia. "Trevia, I know you're upset, but can you please tell me what happened to make you want to go to prison for the rest of your life?"

"Don't you see she's catatonic? She ain't gonna answer you," Denise offered, now standing directly in front of me and Trevia.

"'Nise, shit! Sit down and hush!"

Denise huffed and sat on the other side of Trevia.

I sighed. "Trevia—"

Trevia stopped rocking and looked at me. "He has a wife."

"What?" Denise and I said in unison.

"Wesley is married, has been for six years."

"What?" only Denise said this time.

"And he has two kids, boys."

"How—what?" I asked.

"I knew he would disappear from time to time. Like for weeks at a time. This time he was gone for a month. I thought he was out shacking up with some random chick, not a wife."

Denise glanced at me and asked, "How did you find this out?"

"I followed him to her house, *their* house, one night after a show. Sat my stupid ass out on the parking lot of the Chocolate Playground for hours to see where he would go, because I knew he wouldn't come straight home after work. He never does, even when he's not pulling one of his disappearing acts. Anyway, I followed him there and waited until it was apparent he was spending the night, and then I came home. Went back the next day, but no one was home so I checked the mail, saw mail in his name and in his wife's name—Yolanda Anderson. At first I thought maybe she was some random relative or something. Well, I guess I was just hoping that was it, but it wasn't. I left a note in the mailbox asking her to call me around 11:00 PM, when I knew he'd be at the club."

"And she called you?" I asked.

She nodded. "She did, a week later, and it seems the joke's on me. She's known about me all along. She said they make fun of me because I help Wes with his bills and stuff."

Denise shook her head. "You've been paying his bills?"

That was news to me, too. I knew she liked to buy him things, but paying his bills? Wow.

"Yeah, he told me things were slow at the shows and he wasn't making the tips he used to. He was down, scared he was going to lose his car; he was behind on his credit cards, and I helped him because I loved him and I thought we were working toward something. I feel so damn stupid."

I held up a hand. "Wait, so the wife knew he was with you these three years and she was okay with it?"

"Apparently so," Trevia said through a sniffle. "After she called me a damn fool, she hung up on me."

"When was this call?" Denise inquired.

"Last night or this morning, actually."

"Then why are you trying to go shoot them now?" I asked. "That conversation was hours ago."

"Because Wes called shortly before 'Nise got here yelling at me on the phone about disrespecting his wife. He talked to me like I was a dog, like I have done anything to him besides be good to him, like I knew who this woman was and knowingly slept with her husband. I'm not like that. You guys know I'm not."

Denise and I agreed with her.

"And his wife was in the background yelling about how he'll always be hers. I've met his mother, his brothers and sisters, been to family gatherings, and no one in three years thought to tell me this man was married? I just don't understand." She dissolved into tears and both Denise and I embraced her. I had no idea how bad things were between her and Wesley, and judging from the look on Denise's face, neither did she. Sure, the cheating was evident, but him disappearing for weeks and all that other stuff? I had no clue.

"I'm done. I'm done with him! I'm not taking this crap anymore!" she yelled through her sobs.

I really hoped she meant it.

37

Derek

"What kind of flowers will you be ordering today, Mr. Hill?"

I rested my elbows on my desk and rubbed my forehead. "Um…I don't know. What do you suggest?"

"Well, let's see. We can do another variety of roses. Maybe some miniatures?"

"Yes, whatever you think."

"Okay, and you still want me to vary the colors of the bouquets every hour for twelve hours?"

"Yes."

"Great, we'll get it done."

"Okay, thanks."

I hung up the phone and dug through the side drawer of my desk for a bottle of aspirin. I had to do something about this headache before I passed out or something. By the time I had the aspirins in my hand and was ready to toss them in my mouth, there was a knock at my door.

"Shit," I mumbled, then in a louder voice, grunted out, "Come in!"

Naima, my administrative assistant of more than five years, walked into the room with an expression on her face that read fear and apprehension, but I didn't care.

"Yeah?" I asked.

"Um, here are the contracts you asked me to revise." She just stood there holding the folders in her hand.

"You wanna give them to me or am I supposed to read them from here?"

"Oh…yes, sir." She extended the papers toward me, and I snatched them from her.

I tossed the aspirin into my mouth and took a swig from my water bottle, then noticed she was still in the room. "Is there something else, Naima?"

"No…well…yes, sir. Are you okay? I mean, is there anything else I can do for you?"

"No," I said, my eyes now glued to the contracts.

"Okay. Well, if you need anything…"

I didn't bother to look up until I heard the door close, and then I shut my eyes and reclined in my chair.

It'd been nearly a month since she left me. She wouldn't return my calls. She wouldn't answer my texts. She'd erased me from her life and moved on, and it hurt like hell. Here I was, not sleeping, barely eating. I was a wreck and an asshole to the people around me, and I knew it. Brandon reminded me of it every day, said I was going to run all of our employees off. I didn't care. I was miserable, fucking miserable without Greer, and the hardest part was that I'd always been a fixer. I could come up with a solution to almost anything business-wise. And I thought I had fixed that mess with Sasha. I gave her money, because I knew that was what she wanted, but the whole thing backfired on me.

She took my strategy and used it against me.

Never in a million years did I think she could be that conniving or that she could want to hurt me that deeply, but she did. She ripped my world apart, took away the most important thing in my life, left a damn hole the size of the continent of Africa in my heart. But why? Was she really that upset about us breaking up? Had I underestimated her feelings for me?

I thought about something my father told me when I was a kid. He said if a woman who once loved you tries to kill you, nine times out of ten it means her love was deep, deeper than maybe you even knew. Was that it? Did Sasha love me to the point that she'd want me to hurt like this? Or was she just a twisted crazy person?

I glanced out the window, let my eyes drift to the couch, and saw myself sitting there in the dark with Greer on my lap. Heard the sounds we made together, felt the heat of her body, smelled her perfume. And when the memories were too much, I grabbed my jacket from the back of my chair and left, informing Naima that I wouldn't be back. I had to fix things once and for all.

*****

When she arrived, I fought not to get angry at the sight of her flat stomach. I had to keep my cool and fix this as best I could. I had to do whatever it took to get Greer back.

She slid into the chair across from mine and placed her purse on the table, crossed her long legs just enough for her short skirt to ride up her thighs. Same old Sasha. "Wow, I can't believe you actually came," she said.

"*I* invited *you*, remember?" I replied.

"Yes, well, I'm still recovering from that, too. I can't believe you called me and invited me to dinner." She glanced around the restaurant. "And to my favorite place. I'm totally and completely shocked."

"Well, I figured we needed to talk, to clear the air."

"Why, because your woman left you?"

I cleared my throat and ran a finger around the inside of my shirt collar. "No."

"You're lying, and you're still angry with me. I can tell. I know you, Derek Hill."

"Okay…if you know me, why do you think we're here, Sasha?"

"Hmm, I wanna order before we get down to business. I don't want you backing out of buying me a meal."

"Okay." I told myself to stay calm with her and her games, and then I waved a waiter over to us.

She ordered the most expensive thing on the menu, of course. Despite having zero appetite, I ordered a T-bone.

After our plates were set in front of us, she looked up at me with a smirk, and said, "You're really determined to do this, huh?"

"What do you think I'm trying to do?"

"Get me to help you get that little hood rat of yours back. I mean, those braids?" she scoffed.

"That's what you think?"

She nodded as she cracked open a crab leg. "Yes, and I tell you what. I'll tell her the truth if you write me another check. It was a big sacrifice giving her my check, but I had to convince her I was innocent in all this." She snickered softly. "And she fell for it."

I cleared my throat and shifted in my chair.

"I hated to give up that money, but it was so worth it to see the look on her face and the look on yours right now. You wanna kick my ass, don't you?"

"No."

"Liar."

"Look, I don't want you to tell her anything."

She smiled. "Yes, you do. I told you, I know you, Derek Hill." She dropped the smile. "Unless…are you recording us? Wearing a wire?"

"Really, Sasha? What do you think this is? *Law and Order?*"

She shrugged. You never know…anyway, where was I?"

"You were saying you know me."

"Yes, I do."

"Well, you don't know me as well as you think you do."

"Oh, really?"

"Really. I just want to know why?"

"Why what?"

"Why did you go see her, lie to her? After all I did to help you when you needed it, why?"

She tilted her head to the side. "Help me? You couldn't wait to get me out of your house. And I didn't lie to her. I told her you didn't want a baby with me and that you paid me to get rid of me."

"You also pretended to be pregnant."

She shrugged. "I did that for fun. I liked pretending to be pregnant."

"What was your endgame with the pregnancy? I mean, with me? You would've had to have given birth eventually."

She gave me a pensive look. "I guess I would've had to fake a miscarriage or something. My first plan was to actually get pregnant after I moved in, but as soon as I hit the door you left, and you wouldn't touch me. So I had to take other measures."

"You were going to trap me? Why?"

"Because you're rich. Duh!"

"So all of that crying and shit was an act? It was all about the money?"

"That's what everything is about, Derek."

I took a deep breath and released it. "But why go to all this trouble to hurt me if all you cared about was money? You're attractive. There are other men out there who would gladly take care of you."

"Did I hurt you?"

"Yes, you did. You ruined my relationship with Greer."

"She left you?"

I nodded. "Yes."

"Good. Now you know how it feels for someone you love to dump you over a lie."

"You saying you love me?"

"I'm saying I did."

"Okay…what was the lie?"

"That I cheated on you."

I sighed. I wasn't sure how long I could keep this act up before I went off on her immature ass. "You did cheat, Sasha. I saw you, remember? We had agreed to see each other exclusively. You broke that agreement."

"It's not cheating if you don't really care about the other person."

I leaned forward and watched as she sipped her wine. "Then why sleep with him?"

"First of all, you saw me kiss him, *not* sleep with him. Second of all, if I did sleep with him, maybe it just happened. Maybe he was just there and we just did it. Men do stuff like that all the time. You know, seize the moment, get a little something extra in just for the hell of it. But if a woman does it, she's a slut and a ho' and her dude wants to break shit off and stuff. It's a double standard."

"I never cheated on you, though."

"So you say, but that woman with the weird name sure did pop up out of nowhere. I don't know that you didn't cheat with her."

I couldn't take anymore. She was talking in circles and my headache was slowly returning. "Well, I guess I got my answer. I hurt you and you hurt me back."

She pointed her fork at me. "Right. Now, are you sure we can't negotiate something? How about one hundred thousand this time? I'll call her right now for a hundred thousand. Shit, I'll tell her in person if you want, cry and ask for her forgiveness and everything. I finally got that insurance check and bought me a new place. I need furniture."

I smiled and shook my head. "No. I'm good. I'm gonna go take care of the check. You enjoy your meal."

Her face fell. "You're not staying? You haven't touched your food."

"I've actually got some stuff at work to handle."

"Oh…"

"You take care of yourself, Sasha. Oh, and if you ever step foot on my property again, I'm having your ass arrested for trespassing."

I left the table without waiting for her to reply, found the waiter, and overpaid him for our meals. Then I climbed into my car and was halfway to my house when I made the call. "Did you get it?" I asked. "Could you hear her?"

"Yes, Mr. Hill. I got it, and everything was crystal clear."

38

Greer

I was exhausted, but it was a good kind of exhaustion. Trevia was serious about being done with Wes. Like, dead serious. A few days after her breakdown, he'd actually come back to her, explaining that he and his wife couldn't stand to be around each other for very long and that was why he needed her. Well, she put his ass out. Called the police and everything. And today, a couple of weeks after he showed up, Trevia called me and Denise and asked us to come help her pack his things for his mother to pick up. I was all too glad to do it, even helped load his mother's car. I smiled when she had his mother sign a form she found online as evidence of receipt.

When I asked her if she was okay, she said, "Never better. It's like a new start."

If I didn't need to get back home and start packing for my next trip, I might've drank to that.

I was still sad, but I knew I had to try to get back to my life. In the midst of our break-up, my deal with Sable Jets had expired, and I never responded to Derek's renewal request via email. I would miss the jets and limos, but since they would be a constant reminder of him, it was best I cut that tie.

The flowers were still coming, as evidenced by the notes stuck to my door when I made it back home. I'd missed five deliveries during my time at Trevia's. I shook my head as I pulled them off the door and walked inside, made myself a glass of water, and collapsed onto my sofa. Although it was not quite evening, I was fast asleep in no time and was awakened a little while later by a knock at my door. Figuring it was the flower delivery guy I now knew by name, I answered it with a slight smile. After all, it wasn't Greg's fault Derek was so relentless. Sure enough, it was him with five dozen dahlias in vibrant colors. Yesterday he'd sent miniature roses.

"Thanks," I said after Greg placed them in my living room.

"You're welcome. I don't know what he did, but at this point, even I'm ready to forgive him," the older white man said with a chuckle.

After he left, I looked around the room and sighed. There were so many flowers. Beautiful flowers. I got up to throw away the ones that had wilted, something I did on a daily basis, and my apartment was still full of flowers. The place smelled like a greenhouse or something. I settled back on my couch, picked up my phone, and dialed Derek's number for the first time since our break-up. I was shocked when it went to voicemail. Shocked and even a little insulted, but I left a message nevertheless.

"Derek, it's-uh-Greer. I'm leaving town in a couple of days so you might want to let the florist know. Um, thank you for all of the flowers. Bye."

Well, that was awkward as hell.

No sooner than I hung up, he called back. I couldn't bring myself to answer. I couldn't talk to him. Not yet, because I missed him so much any conversation we had probably would've ended with me back in his bed.

An hour later I checked my mail, and when I made it back to my apartment, was met at the door by the UPS man with a package from Derek. He'd sent letters before, beautiful, heart-wrenching letters. Gifts, too. I figured this small bubble envelope held a combination of both. I opened it to find a short note and a DVD that had no label. The note read:

Greer,

I hope you're doing okay. I'm not. I miss you and I'm becoming a pain in the ass to everyone around me because of it, but I suppose that's my fault. Please watch this DVD, and please call me afterwards.

I love you,
Derek

I grabbed my laptop from my bedroom and had inserted the DVD when a knock came at my door. I checked the time. *Probably poor Greg again,* I thought. I approached the door wondering what color these dahlias would be. I almost fell over when I found Lloyd standing on the other side.

39

Greer

He was wearing his usual suit and tie, and he looked nice. Tired, but nice. I supposed the new baby was keeping him up at night. Trevia had found out it was a little girl.

"Congratulations on your new baby," I said as we both stood on opposite sides of the doorway.

"Um...thanks."

"What's her name?"

"Wow, you know everything, don't you? Her name is Issa."

I nodded. "Nice name."

"Greer, can I come in?"

"Why?"

"Because it's important that I talk to you."

I shook my head. "Lloyd—"

"It's not what you think. I clearly have no chance with you now. It's regrettable, but I get it. Plus, I've got to try to make my marriage work for my daughter, no matter how miserable I am."

I don't know if I felt sorry for him or if I wanted to bask in the fact that he was just as miserable as I was, but for whatever reason, I let him in. His eyes stretched wide when he saw the wall-to-wall flowers.

"I'm guessing my boss is responsible for the new decor?"

I offered him a seat on the bright yellow sofa that he hated, as it was the only suitable seat in the room since I never had sense enough to at least buy an accent chair, and my computer chair was cheap and uncomfortable. I sat as far away from him as I could on the opposite end, and said, "You here to discuss my decor?"

"No." He leaned forward and rested his elbows on his knees, turned his head and looked at me. "I wanted to first give you a proper apology, one with no strings attached."

"Okay. I forgive you. I'm over it, really."

"I know. I'm pretty sure you've been over it for a while."

"I have."

"Good. Because I'm not. You're not so easy to get over, Greer. Not for me. Not for Mr. Hill."

I frowned slightly. "What?"

"I know this is none of my business, and you can curse me and throw me out of here if you want, but just let me say what I need to say."

I didn't reply, just shifted my gaze from him to a bare spot on a wall.

"I don't like him, Greer. Not because he's a bad boss. He's an excellent boss. He's been very accommodating with letting me have extra time off for the baby, and he's been nothing but professional with me despite knowing about us. And I know you told him. I don't like him because you love him."

I crossed my ankles and stared at my feet. Shit, I needed a pedicure in the worst way.

"I know you two broke up, because you haven't been around the office in a while, and plus, that place has a gossiping problem."

I sighed as I returned my attention to his face. "You here to gloat? To throw it in my face?"

"No. I'm here to plead his case."

I sat up straight. "He sent you?" Damn, was Derek that desperate?

"No. I came because I care about you and I want you to be happy. You deserve to be happy, Greer, and I've never seen you as happy as you were with him."

"Are you trying to tell me you're here out of some selfless desire to see me happy? I'm supposed to believe that?"

"It's the truth."

"Well, I don't believe it. I think you want firsthand information about my break-up. You want to see me down and out and miserable. Well, I'm fine, and you can go."

"You're not fine, Greer. You look like you did when we were together—marginally content. You're not happy. He's not happy. Hell, I actually feel sorry for him."

My eyes searched the room as I fought not to care, but I did. "Why? What-what's wrong with him?"

"He looks like he hasn't slept in weeks, and he's short with everyone. His assistant gets the worst of it. The man is losing it. And most of us are afraid he's going to start randomly firing people, and well, I need my job. I *like* my job."

"So that's what this visit is really about? Your job?"

"Partially. Look, he loves you. As much as I hate it, he does. Now, I don't know what happened between the two of you, and I know it's none of my business, but the man is falling apart without you. And from the looks of things around here, he's trying to make it up to you. Just food for thought."

He stood and headed toward my door.

"You drove all the way from Houston to tell me that, or did Derek send you in one of his jets?"

He stopped in his tracks and faced me. "I drove. He doesn't know I'm here. We don't talk about you, Greer. The one time I asked about you a couple of weeks ago, he threatened to fire me if I ever spoke your name again. And he said he'd also kick my ass after he fired me."

I smirked. "Right."

"Look, I know you're going to believe what you want to believe and do what you want to do regardless of anything I say. You've always had a mind of your own."

"And that always bothered you about me, didn't it? That I have a mind of my own?"

He shook his head. "No, Greer. It wasn't that. It was that I never felt like you needed me. I never felt like you needed anyone."

"I need Derek," fell out of my mouth all by itself.

"I know."

As he walked away from my apartment, I said, "Be safe driving back."

"I will."

I stepped back inside of my home, grabbed my laptop, and started the DVD.

40

Greer

I leaned forward as the DVD began to play, and I saw Derek sitting at a table in a restaurant, alone. If the purpose of the video was to make me want and miss him more than I already did, it was working. Lloyd was right, he looked tired, worn even, but he was still my fine, chocolate, dreadlocked Derek and I still loved him. The warm fuzzies I was feeling dropped to the floor and played dead when Sasha entered the frame and took a seat across from him. My eyes narrowed as they spoke to each other, and I noticed something about her I had missed when she came to Derek's house that day—her eyes. There was a callousness in her eyes I had missed, but then again, I was caught totally and completely off guard by her visit. She looked like the kind of woman who loved revenge, the type that specialized in slashing tires and busting windshields, or in other words, wrecking shit. Either she was an excellent actress or I was off my game before, but now I saw it. It was as clear as the nose on my face. She was an A-1 bitch.

Oh, I also noticed her perfectly flat stomach. Either she had given birth and bounced back like a damn champ, or her ass really was lying about being pregnant.

What a bitch!

I watched and listened intently, and the more I heard, the more I wanted to jump through the computer screen and whoop her ass. She'd made a fool of me, had intentionally screwed up my relationship, deceived me into leaving my man, and all of that pissed me the hell off! But I was more upset at myself than anyone for falling for her lies. No, Derek wasn't completely innocent. He definitely should've told me what was going on with her, but after having seen her malicious ass in action, I could see why he didn't. This woman was diabolical.

I grabbed my cell phone to call Derek, having decided not only to forgive him, but to travel to Houston as soon as I could. I didn't want to waste another second apart from him. Then a thought hit me. What if it was all staged? What if Derek paid her to say that stuff?

But it seemed so real. So very real.

I sighed and put the phone down, now thoroughly confused. I watched Derek leave and was just about to stop the DVD when Sasha dug her phone out of her purse and dialed a number. I listened to her end of the conversation and watched the rest of the DVD until the screen went black before changing my clothes and leaving my apartment.

I needed to see Derek.

41

Greer

I was in my car, a half-hour away from home, when I realized I didn't have my cell phone. I started to just keep going, but thought better of it. There was no sense in taking a chance on something happening on the road and without a phone. So I turned around, already a ball of nerves, and was even more on edge by the time I made it back to my apartment, because it took a whole hour to get there! The traffic was especially horrible that evening. And then I got home and was met at the door by Greg, so I had to take the time to let him in and sign for the flowers and tell him I wouldn't be home for the rest of that day or the next. Then I couldn't find my phone, spent twenty minutes searching, and finally found it under a pillow on my couch.

And then I had to pee.

When I stepped out of the bathroom and checked the time, I sighed. I had all of these plans of just showing up at his doorstep and now I was so frustrated, I was a second from giving up and trying again in the morning.

Then out of nowhere, a clap of thunder shook the walls of my apartment and the bottom fell out of the sky. It didn't even look like it was going to rain just a few minutes earlier, let alone storm. This whole thing was truly becoming a comedy of errors. I couldn't recall the last time I left home without my cell phone and now this random-ass thunderstorm? I gave up.

I sat down and dialed his number. I would've preferred our reunion to be face to face, but I needed to talk to him now so I could say what I needed to say before something else crazy happened. When I heard his hello being filtered into my ear through the phone, I melted right then and there. His voice rendered me speechless.

"Hello?" he repeated. "Greer, you there?"

A single tear rolled down my cheek as I said, "Say my name again."

"Oh, baby. Greer. Greer..."

I sucked in a breath and smiled. "I've missed you."

"Baby, I've missed you, too...so much. Thank you. Thank you for calling me."

"I'm sorry I didn't believe you. I watched the video. I saw the end of the DVD. I saw what happened after you left the restaurant."

"Yeah, me too."

"Was that guy, the one she called, the one who took your seat and ate your steak and talked all that shit about you and your money, was he the same man she cheated with?"

"Yep, I don't know who he is, nor do I care to know, but he definitely means more to her than she let on."

"He wasn't too happy about her not getting any money from you."

"Yeah...and he was pissed about her giving you that check without cashing it."

"I really, *really* wanna kick her ass for what she did to you and to us.

I wanna kick both their asses."

"Get in line."

"Derek—how did you record her without her knowing?"

"Paid a private detective to do it. He arrived before I did and set up a hidden camera in the flowers at the table next to ours. I had to pay the waiter to make sure that table remained unoccupied. I even had to wear a mic made to look like a tie clip. I felt like a real spy. It worked out better than I imagined. I was surprised she wasn't more suspicious, but I think she had her mind on trying to get another check out of me, since from what that guy said, that was the point of her agreeing to have dinner with me."

"Derek, I—"

"Wait, baby, I need to say something to you first. I'm sorry about—"

"You already apologized. I get it now. I understand. She's a conniving bitch, and you tried to help her and you didn't tell me everything probably because you thought I wouldn't believe you, and I proved you right when you *did* try to tell me the truth. Look, I don't care about any of that anymore. I just want you back. I want *us* back. Today. Right now."

"You have no idea how it makes me feel to hear you say that. It's like…shit, I can't describe what it feels like to have you back in my life. I love you."

"I love you, too."

"Well, if you love me…let me in, baby. I'm at your door."

Derek

The door flew open and there she stood, just as beautiful as ever, her face wet with tears. She fell into me despite the fact that I was soaking wet from the rain, and wrapped her arms around me.

"You're here," she said into my chest.

"I left Houston right after I missed your first call."

"Did you take one of the jets?"

I smiled down at her. "Of course I did." I peeked inside her apartment. "I see you got the flowers."

She laughed. "Yeah, all ten tons of them."

I squeezed her tightly, closed my eyes at the feel of her softness against my body.

"I'm sorry," she whispered. "I'm sorry, I'm sorry, I'm sorry…"

"I'm sorry, too."

I buried my nose in her hair, inhaled the scents of coconut and shea butter, backed out of her embrace enough to reach down and gently grasp her chin and tilt her head up. She looked into my eyes and kissed me softly. I pressed my lips harder against hers and when she opened her mouth, I dipped my tongue inside and found hers as I lifted her, carrying her into her apartment and kicking the door shut. Setting her down, I backed her against a wall, lifting her hands and pinning them above her head as my mouth devoured hers. The more she moaned, the more I hungered for her. Shit, I was starving for this woman.

I let go of her hands and dropped to my knees in front of her, lifted her blouse and kissed the warm flesh of her stomach before resting my head against it and gripping her waist with my hands. "I love you, baby."

"I love you, too. I love you so much."

I looked up at her as she dug her hands in my dreadlocks. Then I pulled her long skirt down over her hips, letting the fabric fall to her feet.

No panties.

That's my girl.

I smiled as I lifted her left leg and rested it on my right shoulder while she braced herself against the wall. I flicked my tongue across her bud, eliciting a loud moan from her.

Bathing her sex with my tongue, I plunged one finger, then two, inside of her. She grabbed my head, shouted, "Damn, baby!"

For several minutes, I licked and nipped at her clit, pulling it between my lips and suckling it when I felt her right leg buckle. I put my hand on her stomach and felt it quiver. Her body tightened as she screamed my name and spilled all over my fingers.

She got hers.

I was going to make sure she got it again...and again.

Easing her left leg down, I reached for her hand, pulling her onto the floor with me. She snatched her blouse over her head, now totally nude, making my groin ache even more than it already was. With her on her back, I hovered over her and kissed her deeply while she pulled my body onto hers and wrapped her legs around me. I ended the kiss, dragging my mouth from hers to her neck, her chest, and her breasts, taking my time to lavish both with attention. She thrashed beneath me, gasping, moaning, thrusting her sex at me. She was ready for me now, and I was more than ready for her, but I was fighting to keep control, to take my time and love her in a way that she would never forget. This reunion of ours would be one for the record books.

I moved further down her body, dipped my tongue in her navel, and then lifted my body from hers. She reached for me, whispered, "Baby?"

"I'm still here."

I damn near ripped my clothes off while she sat up and watched. She crawled to me, pushed me on my back on the plush orange rug that covered a great part of the floor, dipped her head and caught my left nipple between her teeth. I reached to touch her, but she grabbed my wrists and held them to the floor over my head. She suckled and nipped at my nipples for several minutes before straddling my body and covering my mouth with hers. When she finally let go of my wrists, I rolled us both over, changing the power structure.

I needed to be in control.

She didn't seem to mind at all.

I lifted her legs onto my shoulders, and finding it impossible to hold out any longer, entered her while fixing my eyes on hers. "Ah! Shit, baby!!" I yelled at the sensation of my flesh meeting hers, her juices bathing my shaft.

She clawed at me as I found my rhythm, gliding my length in and out of her wetness.

She felt so good.

Too good.

I made love to her hard and fast, unable to control the pace, my heart racing, my body rocking into hers. I lost count of how many times I told her I loved her and how many times she reciprocated. And when it ended, when my body grew limp from exhaustion, I held her to me, determined to never let her go again.

Greer

We lay there on the floor for hours, sated and spent, naked and dewy with sweat. The scents of the flowers and our sex mingled in the air and I inhaled deeply. I was lying on my back, him on his stomach, his head resting on my belly. I rubbed my hand over his dreadlocks, raking them away from his face with my fingers, caressed his forehead and sighed. My body was tingling from head to toe.

"I love you," he murmured.

I closed my eyes and smiled. "I love you, too. I don't ever want us to be apart again. When you leave here, I'm leaving with you."

He looked up at me. "I know you didn't think I was leaving you here. The only way that can happen is if I move in here with you."

"Hmm, thank you for not giving up on us even when I did."

He moved up my body to face me. "You didn't give up. You accepted the flowers, you never returned any of my gifts, you opened the DVD and watched it. You never gave up on us. And I thank you for that."

"I left my ring at your house, though."

"Oh, yeah." He rolled off of me, reached for his pants, dug in the pocket, and pulled out my ring. "Give me your hand."

As he slid it onto my finger, I said. "Thank you. I'll never take it off again."

"You're welcome, baby."

He lay over my body and brushed his lips across mine. Then he smiled.

"What are you smiling about?" I asked.

He took my hand and placed it on his rock hard penis.

With wide eyes, I said, "Oh…"

42

Greer

Six Months Later

"Damn, stop crying, Trevia! You're not the one getting married," Denise fussed. "This is the last time I'm fixing your make-up."

I shook my head at my two friends. My make-up was done and I was all dressed and ready to go, and although I was getting married in less than thirty minutes, I was cool and calm. It was those two nuts that couldn't seem to get it together.

"Y'all both need to get a grip," I said. "Denise, you're shaking like an Alaskan stripper. Calm down before you have Trevia looking like The Joker."

"Whatever. I don't know why you're so calm. Unless…" She left her post at the make-up table in my suite and walked over to me, giving me a once-over for so long, I started wondering if something was wrong with *my* make-up.

"What?" I asked, looking down at the cream-colored, off-shoulder, formfitting gown that Trevia made for me.

"You got you some this morning, didn't you?"

I gave her a tiny smile.

"Damn, y'all couldn't wait?" Denise asked, throwing her hands up.

I shrugged.

Trevia walked over to us with a half made-up face and her hands on her hips. "I thought y'all had separate rooms?"

"We did. He somehow, accidentally ended up in my room early this morning and my gown just came off by itself, and—"

Denise shook her head. "Uh-uh. I'm not fooling with this heifer today. Come on, Trevia. Let me get you fixed up so we can get this wedding over with. Don't make no sense..."

A few minutes later, a knock at the door signaled it was time for the ceremony to start. There were so many things I was thankful for as I left the room holding a bouquet of white roses with my two best friends flanking me. I was thankful for both of them. I was thankful for this gorgeous destination wedding in Nassau, Bahamas, that I didn't have to plan thanks to Trevia. I was thankful my father was walking me down the aisle. I was thankful for our family and friends who'd traveled from far and near just to see us exchange vows. And as I stepped barefoot onto the white sands of the beach, I was thankful I would be spending the rest of my life loving and making love to the smiling, fine, chocolate, dreadlocked, barefoot man dressed head-to-toe in cream and waiting for me where the sands of the beach met the Atlantic Ocean.

Here's a sneak peek at *Made to Love*, Trevia's story:

1

Trevia

You know your life is careening out of control when you wake up moaning with your love pocket thrumming between your legs.

I'd had another dream, another dream about Wesley Lee Anderson, and Miss Kitty was down there acting a big-time fool. A year after finding out he not only had a wife but two kids that he and his whole family kept hidden from me for the entirety of our three-year relationship, I was still having pornographic dreams about him and his biggie-sized penis. My first error was ever deciding to have sex with him in the first place. My second error was having sex with him more than once that first night, but the first time was so good, I needed another shot of him so I could be sure it wasn't just a fluke.

It wasn't.

Believe me.

So then my third error was trying to turn a hood-famous stripper into a house-husband. It never happened, because dear Wesley had a deeply-rooted vagina addiction. He loved the smell of it, the taste of it, the feel of it, which all worked out to my advantage when he was home. The problem was, his tall, dark, impossibly fine with the huge penis ass was never home. NEVER! So I guess my current situation—being apart from him but desperately wanting him—wasn't so foreign to me. What was different was that I couldn't anticipate his return. I had no expectation of him putting out the fire between my legs.

I sighed and with my eyes still closed, reached over, opened the single drawer of the nightstand, and pulled out what I liked to call my battery-operated helper. Flicked the switch on it and listened to the little motor start, sputter, and die before I could get it under the covers.

Damn-it!

I'd forgotten to replace the batteries.

I threw my helper on the floor, rolled over onto my stomach, and snatched the sticky note that held that morning's affirmation from my mirrored headboard.

"You are worth a world of love. Now get up and go get it."

I crumpled the note up and threw it on the floor, too. It didn't travel as far as my helper. Rolling over onto my back, I stared at the mirrored ceiling, recalled how my dumb ass had had it installed shortly after Wesley moved in so I could see him in action. It was like watching Picasso paint or something. He was a master at sex. I suppose that was why I was still dreaming about it. I suppose that was why I had to fight daily not to call him and request a booty call. Yes, I was addicted to him, emphasis on the *dic*, but I wasn't going to let myself fall into that pit again, the pit where I did all kinds of dumb stuff to make things work with him. Things I'd criticized other women for doing—paying bills, believing lies, actual stalking. I wasn't doing that mess ever again.

Never ever.

I sat up on the side of my bed, scowled at my helper, then reminded myself I had two whole hands full of fingers. Grinning, I headed to the shower to get some relief.

A southern girl at heart, Alexandria House has an affinity for a good banana pudding, Neo Soul music and tall black men in suits. When this fashionista is not shopping, she's writing steamy stories about real black love.

Connect with Alexandria!

Email: msalexhouse@gmail.com

Website: www.msalexhouse.com

Blog: http://msalexhouse.blogspot.com/

Facebook: Alexandria House

Instagram: @msalexhouse

Twitter: @mzalexhouse

www.ingramcontent.com/pod-product-compliance
Lightning Source LLC
Chambersburg PA
CBHW061523020726
47502CB00006B/2207